Shadow of Lies

An Ed Maddux novel

ALSO BY R.J. PATTERSON

Ed Maddux series
  King of Queens
  To Catch a Spy
  Whispers of Treason
  Shadow of Lies

Cal Murphy series
  Dead Shot
  Dead Line
  Better off Dead
  Dead in the Water
  Dead Man's Curve
  Dead and Gone
  Dead Wrong
  Dead Man's Land
  Dead Drop
  Dead to Rights
  Dead End

James Flynn series
  The Warren Omissions
  Imminent Threat
  The Cooper Affair
  Seeds of War

Brady Hawk series
  First Strike
  Deep Cover
  Point of Impact
  Full Blast
  Target Zero
  Fury
  State of Play
  Siege
  Seek and Destroy
  Into the Shadows

Shadow of Lies

An Ed Maddux novel

R.J. PATTERSON

FIRST EDITION

Cover art by Dan Pitts.

A truth that's told with bad intent
beats all the lies you can invent.
— WILLIAM BLAKE

May 1956, Rosario, Argentina

DR. HEINRICH SCHWARZ GLANCED over his shoulder as he walked down the street, a habit developed from his survival instinct. Clutching his wife's hand, he urged his three daughters forward along the sidewalk. Church bells chimed from the belfry looming over them just outside the Iglesia San Antonio, signaling the end of another service. Listening to homilies delivered in Spanish rather than German was still awkward, but after nearly a decade of living in Argentina, he was getting more comfortable with it just like everything else. But he didn't think he would ever get comfortable living in a constant state of angst.

"What is it, dear?" his wife, Clara, asked. "Was it something Father Lopez said?"

He shook his head and kept walking.

"Well, what is it then? It's clear that something is bothering you."

"Let's talk about it later at home."

He stole a look over his shoulder once more, confirming his suspicions.

Thousands of miles from his homeland, such

precautions were necessary to protect his family as well as his own life. People wanted him dead for his association with the Nazis. If subjected to a trial, they wouldn't care about the fact that he was forced into service. Serving under duress wouldn't weigh in the judge's or jury's decision. They would simply see a picture of him with that swastika armband on his jacket, a symbol that was detested worldwide. They wouldn't see his humanity or consider the fate of his wife and daughters. A pronouncement of guilty would precede a swinging gavel and a swift death sentence.

"No, Heinrich," his wife said, coming to a full stop before stamping her foot. "I want to talk about it right now."

He never let go of his wife's hand as he kept walking. Once her arm was fully extended, he jerked her toward him, resulting in her stumbling a few feet before regaining her balance.

"What are you doing?" she demanded.

"They're here. And if we don't hurry, this might be the end of our family as we know it. I know what they'll do to me, but God knows how they'll treat you and the girls. I'm not interested in finding out either."

They hustled through Alem Park and toward the sailing club that held his boat.

"Papa, why do we have to run? Why can't we enjoy the sunshine on our walk?" asked Anna, his youngest daughter.

"We're going sailing, dear," Schwarz said. "But we need to hurry up."

"Why do you keep looking over your shoulder?" she asked.

"Just keep moving."

When the Paraná River came into view, Schwarz urged on the rest of his family. A quick glance behind him let him know that he wasn't imagining anything. Three men in suits were following them and had abandoned any semblance of being on a casual walk. Schwarz knew he'd finally been found—but he wasn't shocked. He knew eventually someone would track him down. Yet he wasn't about to go down without a fight.

In preparation for such an event, Schwarz had several plans to escape if this moment ever arrived. He had bags with clothes and money in his car and his boat to help ease the transition. But that wasn't all. In anticipation of having to start over somewhere, he also squirreled away money in international banks that he could access eventually without alerting any authorities.

"Papa, I'm scared," Anna said.

"Everything will be fine," Schwarz said. "We're almost there."

With one final look behind, Schwarz estimated how long he would have to get the boat away from the dock and moving onto the river. He wouldn't have much time, but he knew he could do it if he hurried.

"Everyone, run," he said as he broke into a sprint.

He raced down the dock toward his boat, *La Libertad*, and began removing the ropes from the dock cleats. His oldest daughter, Katarina, rushed to assist him, firing up the engine. The motor sputtered for a moment before roaring to life. The water churned beneath the propellers.

Clara snatched up Anna and carried her across the dock while prodding their middle child, Maria, forward.

Once they reached the boat, Clara handed her husband Anna, while he held out his hand to help Clara and Maria inside. With everyone safely aboard, he rushed over to the helm and spun the wheel toward the center of the channel as he thrust the throttle open.

Schwarz looked back in time to see three men standing on the edge of the dock, hands on their hips and breathing heavily. He smiled as he turned his attention to the canal in front of him before Clara and his three daughters started screaming for him to stop.

Schwarz swerved to his right as a boat churned straight toward them. With two children swimming off the edge of the dock in front of him, he was forced to slow down to avoid them. When he did, another boat about fifty meters ahead of them eased into the canal, blocking all access.

Narrowing his eyes, Schwarz punched the horn several times before waving for the boat to move aside. The boat didn't move.

Schwarz unleashed a slew of German curse words as he directed a steely gaze toward the other captain. The man sauntered out from the helm and walked up to the port side. Propping his knee up on the edge, the captain puffed on a cigar. When he pulled it out of his mouth, a wide grin spread across his face.

Without any other options, Schwarz was forced to slow down to avoid a direct collision. He eased off the gas, throwing the boat into reverse.

"Get below," Schwarz said without even looking at Clara.

"What's going on?" she asked.

"Get below now," he said gruffly.

She gathered up the girls and ushered them below deck, disappearing from Schwarz's sight.

Schwarz put the engine in neutral and drifted slowly toward the vessel impeding his path.

"Can I help you?" Schwarz asked tersely.

"Well, Dr. Schwarz, I believe you can," the other man said.

He jammed his cigar back into his mouth and took several more puffs.

Schwarz eyed the man closely.

"I don't know who you are, but I suggest you get out of my way."

"Is that how you've always handled those who tried to stop you in the past? You just intimidate them by threatening to run them over? Well, newsflash for you, Mr. Nazi Scientist Man, my boat is bigger than yours— and you can't intimidate me."

Schwarz reached beneath the wheel and grabbed a pistol before training it on the man.

The man didn't flinch, instead wagging his finger and clucking his tongue.

"I'd reconsider that move if I were you," he said. "If you take a moment to look behind you, you'll see several of my men bearing down on your position. You also probably didn't notice the two snipers I have on board my ship who have you in their sights right now. If you so much as flinch, you'll be dead before you hit the water. And I'd hate for a good family man like your-self to go like that in front of your wife and children."

Schwarz shook his gun at the man, keeping it trained on him.

"I'm not going to fall for that trap," Schwarz said.

"It's not a trap, Doc. I deal in absolutes, not deceptive tactics."

The water lapped hard against the side of *La Libertad* as Schwarz considered his options. A quick peek over his shoulder let him know that the man was indeed telling the truth. The three men dressed in suits who had looked defeated just moments earlier were charging hard toward him in a small boat.

Schwarz's options were rapidly disappearing. He didn't want his children to be subjected to lies in the media about what kind of man he was. He also didn't want them to watch him get shot to death. But with the other boat closing in, he had to choose between one of those two options.

He swallowed hard and prepared to do something he'd never done in his life—kill another man.

But before he could pull the trigger, he felt a sharp prick in his neck. Next, his vision went blurry and his legs weak before he crumpled to the deck.

* * *

A HALF HOUR LATER, Schwarz regained consciousness in a bed located in the bowels of an unfamiliar boat. The vessel rocked gently, and seagulls called outside. He eased onto his feet and crept toward the door. Jiggling the handle, he found it locked.

"Boss," a man on the other side of the door called, "he's awake."

Thundering footsteps rushed down the hall before falling silent. Schwarz slipped behind the wall and prepared for a fight.

As soon as the door swung wide open, Schwarz tried to hit the first entrant in the head with it, but the attempt failed miserably. Within ten seconds, two additional men rushed into the room and subdued Schwarz.

"Settle down," said the man who'd stood at the helm of the boat that had blocked *La Libertad*. "If you get rowdy again, I might have to put you down for another nap."

"Where's my family?" Schwarz demanded as he walked backward toward the bed.

"They're fine," the man said. "We're not here to hurt you."

"Your actions say otherwise."

"Do they? You aren't bleeding, are you? Any broken bones? Sore from any beating? I think we've done a pretty good job of proving that exacting a pound of flesh isn't on our agenda."

Schwarz exhaled slowly and took a seat on the bed. "So, what is it that you want exactly?"

"Probably something you never imagined you'd get—your freedom."

Schwarz forced a chuckle. "And who are you exactly? I wasn't aware there were arbiters of justice who could grant such things."

"My name is Terry Fulbright, and I work for the CIA. I've been authorized to bring you back to the U.S. where you can start afresh, working in your field again instead of simply teaching physics at some high school in Argentina. I'm sure you would prefer to live free without having to look over your shoulder."

Schwarz narrowed his eyes and glared at Fulbright.

"Nothing will ever change that, even if I live to be a hundred years old."

Fulbright shrugged. "If you're not interested, we

could leave you alone and let you gamble that no one will find you. However, your wife seemed excited about the prospect of you returning with us."

Schwarz leapt to his feet.

"You better not have hurt her," he said as he poked Fulbright in the chest.

Fulbright took Schwarz's hand and shoved it away.

"I would never hurt your wife and children," Fulbright said. "I'm trying to convince you to come back with me. And that wouldn't exactly help my cause, would it?"

"I want to see my wife," Schwarz said.

"After you give me your answer."

"What's the catch? There's always a catch."

"If you consider being granted a new alias so that no Nazi hunter will find you and getting a position within the U.S.'s National Advisory Committee for Aeronautics a catch, I guess that's it. Otherwise, there isn't one. We help you now, and you help us later."

"And my children?"

"They'll be there with you in Hampton, Virginia, attending the best schools available while you work at the Langley Aeronautical Lab and help our scientists solve their rocket propulsion problems."

"Rocket propulsion? How fast do you want to go?"

Fulbright wagged his finger. "It's not how fast we want to go, but how far."

"What are you trying to do? Fly to the moon?"

"That's exactly what we're trying to do. Now, I think I've given you a picture of what your life could be like. And I doubt you'd prefer to continue teaching high school level courses to a bunch of uninterested kids rather than continuing to conduct cutting-edge research. But I'll leave you alone to think about it and make that decision. You have five minutes."

Before Fulbright closed the door, Schwarz stopped him.

"I don't need five minutes," he said. "I'll do it."

Fulbright smiled and offered his hand to Schwarz.

"In that case, welcome to the greatest country on Earth, Dr. Schwarz."

NOVEMBER 8, 1965, BONN, GERMANY

WHILE STOPPED AT A TRAFFIC LIGHT, Günter Voigt lowered the volume on his transistor radio unit before adjusting his earpiece to fit more comfortably. He waited until the men seated behind him began talking about important things before recording their conversation. Talk of FC Cologne's chances of winning the German soccer league persisted until one of the men mentioned that they needed to get on with their business before they ran out of time.

Voigt pulled up to a hotel and put the car in park. His job as a chauffeur for the KGB in Bonn was both painful yet necessary. With his wife and two children remaining in East Berlin, he couldn't pass up the opportunity to get work where he could. Yet when the KGB invited him to serve as their chauffeur, he realized it wasn't really a question.

A train engineer by trade, Voigt lost his job when the Russians began to form a closer alliance with the East Germans. Russia wanted to control the rail lines throughout Eastern Europe and exerted pressure on neighboring countries regarding who was fit to ferry sensitive shipments back and forth. Voigt had barely been working in his position for less than a year and didn't make the cut. But in an effort not to leave the dismissed engineers in an economic quagmire, the Russians extended them job offers in various other fields.

And while the argument could be made that the job was essentially the same—transporting people from one place to another—Voigt felt like his skills were being wasted.

"What is the score?" one of the men from the back seat asked.

"Nil-nil," Voigt said.

"How's your wife?" asked Sasha Ivanov, the other passenger and the Russian ambassador here.

"She's about to bust, but she's healthy, which is the most important thing."

Voigt only had one more day on his shift before he would return home for a week to be with his wife. Neither of them wanted any more children since they struggled to provide for the ones they had. But they couldn't exactly help themselves after being separated for so long. However, Voigt refused to call his wife's latest pregnancy an accident. It just wasn't optimal timing, especially with finances so tight.

He also assumed that's why he was such a solid candidate for recruitment by the CIA.

When Voigt first met Malcolm Poindexter, their encounter seemed like a chance meeting. But Voigt realized that wasn't the case; instead, it had been planned out for a while with great attention to detail. The location was in a pub, a noisy one that he frequented every Friday evening. Voigt realized that was when his mental state was at its lowest. He had reached the weekend, the time he used to look forward to spending with his family but instead was wasted drinking beer and longing to be anywhere else.

Poindexter slid onto the stool next to Voigt and started up a conversation about soccer. The talk then drifted toward family. Voigt's mental state spiraled downward before his new friend offered him hope.

"What if I told you that I could solve your financial problems, maybe even help you save enough to start a new life at some point?" Poindexter had asked Voigt.

"I'm listening."

"You hear things, don't you?"

Voigt furrowed his brow. "What do you mean?"

"On your job—you drive around important people, right?"

Voigt eyed the man closely. "Who are you?"

"Let's just say I'm not on the same side as the people you drive around. And I'd make it worth your while financially if you just so happen to hear something they say and then you share it with me. It's really just that simple."

That was the moment Voigt realized this wasn't some random stranger. This was a set up, but Voigt also couldn't refuse the offer. Accepting it was risky but laden with rewards. The money was enticing only because of the opportunity that it could afford him and his family. Perhaps a new start somewhere else, a place where he could do more than chauffeur important people around, a place where maybe he could be significant.

Two days after his initial meeting with Poindexter, Voigt found a payphone and dialed the number on the card he'd been given. A week later, the protocol had been set up for sharing information and for receiving the cash.

"What are you waiting on?" Ivanov said, snapping Voigt back to the present. "The light is green."

Voigt nodded and apologized before accelerating. Whenever he was transporting high-ranking Russian diplomats, he had to be extra careful to make sure no one was following him. His route was always given to him just before he slipped into the driver's seat, and today was no exception. However, there was always one busy intersection on the route, one he could always count on being stopped at for at least a minute.

With the light turning from yellow to red, Voigt eased onto the brake, forcing the car to stop.

"Why is there so much traffic today?" groused the other man in the back.

Voigt adjusted his sunglasses and then flashed a quick thumbs up as he gripped the steering wheel. The move was subtle, so nonchalant that hardly anyone would notice unless they were watching for it.

But someone was watching.

III

ED MADDUX STRETCHED FORWARD and then pulled back hard on the oars as his rhythmic movements rushed him along the Rhine River. He ignored the bitter wind biting against his face, lost in thought. Moving to Europe had proved to be adventuresome in ways he'd never imagined, particularly when it came to his fledgling role with the CIA. But the position had blossomed into so much more due to his job with Opel. With the ability to move freely between countries without drawing much suspicion, he had become an important asset for the agency, solidifying his place at the Bonn station in Germany.

Over the past few weeks, the CIA activity that had kept him busy allowed him time to return to the water. However, as much as he enjoyed skimming across the Rhine, he was itching to return to the field.

After an hour, he rowed to the dock and put up his boat. Following a quick shower at the Bonn Boating Club, he hustled over to the CIA offices to check in with the station chief, Charles Pritchett.

When Maddux reached Pritchett's office, he wasn't there.

"If you're looking for Pritchett, he's down the hall in a meeting," a woman said.

Maddux spun around to see Rose Fuller, whose head was down, engrossed in fiddling with a mechanical gadget. He smiled as he caught sight of her.

"Is this your latest technological innovation?" he asked.

"Hardly," she said as she looked up at him. "It's a switch that's acting up. I think it's got some corrosion on here that's keeping it from working properly."

"I'm sure you'll figure it out. You always do."

She forced a smile and shook her head before studying the object closely again.

"If you could only see the table I call 'The Grave-yard' in my lab. It's got more failed ideas than you could imagine sprawled everywhere. It's truly a mess and proof that I'm not close to being the genius you make me out to be."

"I'm sure it's simply a field of dormant ideas waiting to be activated by that brilliant mind of yours," he said.

She waved at him dismissively.

"Oh, stop flattering me," she said before putting her hand up to the side of her mouth and whispering, "If you keep this up, people might get the wrong idea about us."

Maddux froze for a moment, unsure of what she meant.

Then she winked.

Maddux sighed and huffed a laugh through his nose.

"You had me there for a minute," he said before he turned and headed down the hall.

"Before you go barging in on that meeting, there's one more thing you ought to know," she said.

Maddux stopped and whipped back around in her direction. "And that is?"

"Make sure you ask Pritchett about the file he has for you," she said. "I'm sure you'll find it interesting, to say the least."

He nodded and resumed his march toward Pritchett. Maddux knocked softly and eased the door open, refusing to wait for permission to enter.

Pritchett shook his head and looked down. "Maddux, this meeting doesn't concern you."

"I'm sure it doesn't, but I'm having espionage withdrawal," Maddux said. "I need something to do, or I'm gonna go crazy."

Pritchett adjusted the patch over his right eye and then gestured toward the seat at the end of the table, opposite of him. "Just have a seat, and keep your mouth shut."

Maddux nodded and slipped into the chair. Pritchett sat at the far end of the long conference room table, his legs crossed, his only hand clasped over his hook and resting on his knee. Agents Malcolm Poindexter and Terry Fulbright sat to Pritchett's left and right, respectively.

Pritchett returned his attention to Poindexter, who also went by Dex.

"And what do you make of CAShadow-5?" Pritchett asked.

"I don't think there's any reason to worry about him," Dex said. "He's being forced to work for the KGB and is separated from his family. He's barely being paid a livable wage while laboring under the threat of being separated from his wife and children at any moment."

"That's what makes me all the more worried," Pritchett said. "If he feels backed into a corner, he might turn the tables on us."

Fulbright shook his head. "No way. I recruited him because of what the KGB had done to him. We can sit here all day and psychoanalyze him, but the fact remains that he wants to provide for his family, and that's barely happening as is. Not to mention, the bigger motivating factor for CAShadow-5 to help us in the first place had to do more with principle than anything. He hates the commies and how they've ruined his country."

"He'd leave if he could," Dex added, "but he's a good family man. He wouldn't do such a thing without taking his family with him. And that's not about to happen in the foreseeable future."

Pritchett uncoiled and pulled his chair closer to the table. He used his hook to reach a sheet of paper far out in front of him. He studied the document for a moment.

"You might be right," Pritchett said. "But how much good intel is he giving us? And can we be sure he's not serving as a double agent?"

"If he is a double agent, he's not getting anything from us," Dex said. "Our conversations with him are strictly one way."

"And the intel he's delivered so far?"

Fulbright crossed his arms and leaned back in his seat. "So far, he's proved to be incredibly valuable. We've been able to glean some information from conversations between several foreign diplomats and Ivanov, the so-called ambassador that CAShadow-5 is driving around."

"And what about today's operation?" Pritchett asked.

"It's not too complicated," Dex said. "Ivanov is meeting with a man we've identified as a top director within the KGB, Tamryn Zhutov. We want to listen in on their discussion."

"And what do we know about the nature of this meeting?" Pritchett asked.

"At the moment, nothing," Fulbright said. "But when we intercepted a dispatch about this proposed meeting, we learned that CAShadow-5 would be involved and we wanted him to lead us right to the site."

"Why not just meet at the embassy?" Pritchett asked. "They could have all the privacy they wanted there."

"Zhutov is suspicious by nature," Dex said. "Everything he does is unpredictable, evidenced by the fact that he flips a coin to decide where to go and what to do on certain decisions. He doesn't ever want to fall into a pattern."

Pritchett arched an eyebrow. "And you think your guy is going to take him to some random place that hasn't been vetted and swept for any kind of eavesdropping technology?"

"No," Dex said. "There are exactly five places they could end up, but we don't have the manpower to stake them all out safely. So, we have a different plan."

"Which is?"

"We're going to tail CAShadow-5 to the location," Fulbright said.

Pritchett started laughing. "And to think I consider you two some of my best agents. You honestly think you won't be spotted? This meeting is occurring this afternoon in broad daylight for precisely the reason that no one will be able to follow them without being identified."

"That's why we have a backup plan," Fulbright said with a wink.

Pritchett cocked his head to one side as a smile crept across his face. He wagged his index finger at Fulbright.

"You're redeeming my faith in you—almost," Pritchett said. "What's this backup plan look like?"

"If we get separated, CAShadow-5 has a device he can activate that will lead us right to his position."

"Why wasn't that the plan all along? Seems a lot less riskier."

"We need to be within a five-mile radius for it to work," Dex said. "Rose said it might work within a six-mile radius, but she hasn't been able to get it to consistently work from that distance."

"This doesn't sound like a backup plan as much as a Hail Mary if you get made while tailing him," Pritchett said.

Fulbright shrugged. "Surely we'd prefer other methods, but given the situation, we had to work with what we had. Besides, Rose is a whiz when it comes to this kind of technology. I wouldn't suggest anything she creates to be along the lines of a Hail Mary. Isn't that right, Maddux?"

The blood rushed to Maddux's face. He hoped the crimson hue didn't look as obvious as it felt. He nodded as he thought of something to say to deflect the attention. "I've found her gadgets to be quite helpful."

"I bet you have," Fulbright said with a snicker.

Pritchett sighed, ignoring the jab. "I don't need agents vouching for Rose's work. I simply need results. Now, I hope you're right about CAShadow-5. Because if you're wrong, we may miss a big opportunity to find out what Zhutov is doing here and what the KGB's plans might be."

Dex nodded. "I'm confident you'll be pleasantly surprised."

"What time is this going to happen?"

"In about an hour," Fulbright said.

"I'd love to join you," Maddux said.

Pritchett shook his head. "Absolutely not. You don't need to get involved in these types of operations."

"You mean the kind where I get shot at and maybe even have my cover blown?" Maddux said. "It's too late for that."

"Don't give me any grief over this, Maddux. Besides, I have something that I think you'll find more interesting on a personal level once we're done here."

"Anything else we need to know before we leave?" Dex asked.

"Yes, one more thing," Pritchett said. "The Berlin station chief said he's been unable to get anything out of Alexander Buturovich, one of the KGB's top spies. They plan on moving him soon."

"And we're going to be involved with that, I assume," Fulbright said.

"Most likely, but I'll keep you posted on that. Director Raborn wants Buturovich on U.S. soil, and the transfer is going to take place within the next couple of days. Apparently, Washington has other ideas for him."

Pritchett wished Dex and Fulbright good luck then dismissed them before inviting Maddux to the other end of the table.

"What is it?" Maddux asked.

Pritchett searched through the pile of papers in front of him before sliding out a manila folder and handing it to Maddux.

"Everything you want to know about Gil Williams," Pritchett said.

Maddux nodded as he began to sift through the document.

"I already went through it," Pritchett said. "I'll give you the highlights."

Maddux closed the folder and sat back. "I'm listening."

"I promised you this information, but it's important that I let you know I worked with Gil in the past. It wasn't on any major operation, but I knew him somewhat, and I never suspected he might be working for the Russians."

"He's a traitor?"

"That's open to interpretation, but here's what you need to know about Williams. When he retired from the agency several years ago in Barcelona, he was serving as the CIA station chief in Moscow. But even more poignant was the fact that he was suspected of smuggling weapons into Russia, including some U.S. military state-of-the-art technology."

"And now he just walks free?"

"From what I understand and read in those files, Williams appears to have ceased all suspicious activity."

Maddux glanced at the files for a moment before

closing it. "These don't look like official reports," he said. "They appear to be the work of an agent who had a hunch, but nothing seems official."

"I had to call in a few favors to get this information for you, so it may not have gone through all the proper channels, if you understand what I'm saying."

Maddux nodded. "You got what you could, but you have no idea if any of this has been verified. It's just some reservations about Williams expressed by an agent or two. Who knows what he could've really been up to."

"That's what I like about you, Maddux. Nothing ever gets by you."

Maddux arched his eyebrows. "Were you trying to get something past me?"

Pritchett scowled. "Of course not. I simply wanted to follow through on my promise and, to be completely honest with you, I had a hard time coming up with anything. All his files are restricted, viewable only by a security clearance much higher than mine."

"If a station chief was helping smuggle technology into the country of our greatest enemy, you'd think this would be more widespread knowledge and certainly not hidden away. Either someone's protecting him—"

"Or someone is protecting him."

"What do you mean?"

Pritchett shifted in his seat and then leaned forward. "What I mean is maybe there's more to the story than what was unearthed in this report."

"Which means you don't know anything definitive about him," Maddux said. "Williams could be a traitor or a patriot, leaving us without any threads to pull on."

"Agents are reticent to accuse their own unless the

proof is undeniable. And as you may have already figured out, in our field, obtaining definitive proof is one of the most difficult challenges we face." Pritchett stood up. "But dig through those files," he said. "Maybe you'll see something I missed."

After Pritchett left the room, Maddux sifted through several reports and eventually came across a handful of pictures of Williams posing with other agents and dignitaries. In one of the photos, Williams was clutching a book with the spine barely visible. Maddux squinted as he tried to make out the title, which had a black mark along the edge.

"*The Last Hurrah*," he mumbled to himself.

But that wasn't all that interested Maddux in the picture. Williams had his arm around another man who looked vaguely familiar.

Where have I seen that guy?

Maddux tucked the photo into his coat pocket and closed the folder. He planned to dig into the documents more later that evening.

* * *

DEX TOOK ANOTHER DRAG from his cigarette before he flicked it through the open window on the driver's side. He glanced over at Fulbright, who was on his third cup of coffee since they started waiting.

"I don't know how you do it," Dex said.

"Do what? Look this incredibly handsome?"

Dex huffed a laugh. "No, you don't do that at all. I was wondering how you can drink that much coffee while we're waiting for someone. If that were me, my bladder would explode."

Fulbright shook his head and smiled. "I'm quite

certain that what runs through my veins is a fifty-fifty mix of coffee and blood. My body absorbs it."

Dex tapped his watch and observed another steady stream of cars flood the intersection.

"How are we even gonna see him with all this traffic?" Fulbright asked.

"He knows what he's doing," Dex said. "Isn't that why you recruited him in the first place?"

Fulbright shrugged. "That may have had a little to do with it. But to be frank, I mostly recruited him because of his unfettered access to the top-level directors within the KGB."

After another minute of silence, CAShadow-5's car rolled to a stop at the intersection.

"Is that him?" Dex asked.

"The one and only."

CAShadow-5 wore a pair of sunglasses and a three-piece suit. He worked on a piece of gum before giving the signal. After adjusting his sunglasses, he flashed a thumbs-up sign.

"Keep your distance," Fulbright warned as they started to follow the car. "We don't want to blow this thing. If we're able to get this information, this moment could make our careers."

"It could also end with us getting shot in the head."

"You're just a ray of sunshine, aren't you?"

"I try."

Dex stomped on the gas as he tried to keep pace in traffic. He came upon a light that was yellow and about to turn red, increasing his speed to get through the intersection.

"If someone is watching for them, we're blown

after that last maneuver," Fulbright said.

"If I didn't, we would've lost them. I'd rather take my chances because losing our cover isn't a done deal. But if we're blown, we're blown."

Fulbright frowned and sighed. "I've got a bad feeling about this."

Dex watched as CAShadow-5 put on his blinker and turned right down a side street. Following suit, Dex eased around the corner and started to panic.

"Where is he?" Fulbright asked as he leaned forward and peered down the street.

"I—I don't know," Dex said. "It's like he vanished into thin air."

Dex sped along the road as he and Fulbright checked for the car careening along one of the adjacent streets.

"You see anything?" Dex asked.

"Nothing," Fulbright said. "He's gone."

Dex pounded his fist on the dashboard. "Maybe Pritchett was right."

IV

GÜNTER VOIGT WOVE IN and out of traffic as he attempted to lose the pair of CIA agents on his tail. He had ferried Ivanov all over Bonn enough to know where the best side streets and intersections to ditch a trailing spy. Yet Voigt's driving skills weren't enough to keep him from getting scolded.

"What are you doing?" Ivanov asked. "Did you see those two men following us?"

Voigt nodded, keeping his hands on the steering wheel and eyes on the road.

"You know better than that," Ivanov said. "No one should ever follow us for that long."

"I'm sorry," Voigt said. "I was a little distracted."

"From the game?"

Voigt nodded.

"Then put the radio away."

Voigt came to a stop at a traffic light before complying with Ivanov's request.

"I expect more out of you," Ivanov said. "These are dangerous times for us. The Americans will be relentless in their pursuit of our people. Like it or not, you are one of us now, and you can't drop your guard, not even for a second."

Voigt nodded knowingly and adjusted the rearview mirror so he could see Ivanov better. His deputy, Yuri Sokolov, stared out the window. Both men appeared anxious to Voigt.

"Everything will be fine," Voigt said. "I lost them several blocks back. They won't be able to find us."

"That's not what I'm worried about," Ivanov said, resisting Voigt's attempts to assuage him.

Sokolov turned to Ivanov and spoke in hushed tones, but it was still loud enough for Voigt to hear everything.

"Your plan is going to work. We just need to be patient and let it develop slowly. You know we can't rush an operation like this."

Ivanov sighed. "And therein lies our biggest challenge. The world of espionage is changing so rapidly that we can't wait for our technology and our methods to catch up with what everyone else is doing. We must be the innovators."

"Or we must be the ones patient enough to let everything unfold over time," Sokolov said. "The long game is far more effective. We must be committed to this path."

"Yet it is fraught with danger."

"Such as?"

Ivanov turned toward the window. "There is an equal chance that nothing comes of what we're doing. And then what? We've put ourselves backward ten years in a field that is already ten years ahead of the rest of the world. The risk is great."

"So is the reward."

"I'm afraid that your faith in this program is shared by Zhutov. He's going to back this plan without any reservations."

"Operation Iron Eagle is already being implemented. Last week, the first batch of agents were inserted into the U.S. for strategic purposes."

"You think our agency is smart enough to project who exactly will be running the U.S. government in the next ten or fifteen years, especially someone who isn't even in politics yet? Because you know the current politicians have a heightened awareness about affiliating with any Russian. McCarthyism still thrives in the U.S., especially when it can be used as a political weapon."

"The agents we're sending could fool even you," Sokolov said. "You would think they were born in a New York City borough and grew up rooting for the Yankees. If there's even a hint of their accent remaining, they can't be deployed."

"And you sincerely believe our agents will be able to avoid any suspicion after they're thrust into the U.S.?"

"The United States isn't like the motherland," Sokolov said. "You know that. People don't share the same distrust we do and wouldn't contact the local authorities about a neighbor unless he was doing something illegal."

Ivanov shook his head slowly. "I just don't see there being much of a chance to succeed. There's nothing wrong with the process we've been using."

"Except for the fact that it hasn't been all that effective. Look, I get it—pummeling American spies is fun. Who doesn't love to beat information out of their enemy? But the quality of information we get is oftentimes too old to be useful or used to deflect our attention away from where it needs to be."

"I like the way it used to be when times were simpler. It was easier to manage my spies."

Sokolov shrugged. "Unless you have a time machine, you're stuck in the rapidly developing present. Technology, ideas, politics—it's moving so fast that it's becoming a blur. But if you think that how you do things now is going to be effective a year from now or even six months, you're going to find yourself at the Kremlin pushing papers."

Ivanov cut his eyes toward Sokolov. "If I didn't know any better, you sound like someone after my position."

"You're the master," Sokolov said. "I chose this post so I could learn from the best. And I hope that you continue to be the creative intelligence officer who has kept us one step ahead of the Americans."

Voigt eased onto the brakes, bringing the car to a halt just outside a warehouse. Based on the rotting pallets and rusted barrels strewn haphazardly across the grounds, he figured no one had used the facility in at least several years.

"We're here," he said.

Ivanov didn't move, sharing one final thought with Sokolov. "It's not easy to stay ahead in this business, but perhaps you're right. Maybe the only thing that will work as the future races toward us are assets properly placed behind enemy lines who can strike for us when the time is right."

Ivanov adjusted his tie before opening the door. He climbed out, shut the door behind him, and then strode toward a door at the corner of the building.

Voigt watched the KGB leader disappear inside.

"That was quite a pitch," Voigt said as he turned toward the back and looked at Sokolov.

"It was all true."

"Really? All of it?"

Sokolov nodded. "Ivanov needs to know that his methods are going extinct. It won't be long before all of the information he's been sitting on will be effectively obsolete."

"So, you are after his job?"

Sokolov pulled his gun out and inspected the barrel.

"Why don't you just do yours?" he said before exiting the vehicle.

Voigt sat still, waiting until Sokolov had vanished into the building. Once he was inside, Voigt hustled out of his car and unlocked the trunk. He used his key to pry open a small hatch built into the sidewall. Plunging his hand into the opening, he felt around until he secured a firm grip on the box. He pulled it out and then shut the trunk before hustling toward a set of fire escape stairs ascending along the outside of the warehouse.

Kneeling, Voigt used the steps as a shield from any prying eyes. He didn't want anyone to see him, let alone mistake him for someone else.

Without wasting any time, he opened the box and assembled the unit he'd received from his CIA contact. Voigt connected several pieces and proceeded to hook up the battery, which weighed as much if not more than the entire device itself. A green light flickered on, signaling that the transmitter was operational.

Voigt took a deep breath before pushing the button that activated the beacon. There was no noise, not even the faint sound of a beep or the low hum of an electrical current. And only someone with the corresponding receiver could pinpoint the exact location of the device.

Voigt hustled back to his car and then slipped behind the steering wheel.

Less than two minutes later, Ivanov emerged from the building and lumbered back toward the vehicle. He passed by the front of it and headed straight for the driver's side. Using his finger, he motioned for Voigt to roll down his window.

"Did you set up the beacon?" Ivanov asked.

Voigt nodded.

A hint of a smile appeared around the corners of Ivanov's mouth.

"Good work, comrade. Just make sure you get some place safe in case a gunfight breaks out. I'd hate for you to get caught in the crossfire."

"I hope that nothing of the sort transpires."

"That makes two of us."

Voigt cranked the engine and eased the vehicle to the far end of the parking lot.

All he could do now was wait.

V

DEX WHEELED HIS CAR into a grocery store parking lot and then came to an abrupt stop. He threw his head back and let out a long sigh before loosening his tie. After scanning the area in front of him for a few minutes, he closed his eyes and shook his head slowly.

"What exactly are we doing here?" Fulbright asked.

"I need some smokes," Dex said. He opened the door and eased out.

As Dex walked around the other side of the vehicle, Fulbright rolled his window down and threw a dollar at him.

"Pick me up a pack too, will ya?" Fulbright said.

"You good with Marlboros?" Dex asked as he picked the bill up off the ground.

"I prefer Lucky Strikes," Fulbright said. "Marlboros are still mild as May in my book."

"You and Maddux are two peas in a pod," Dex said. "You and your silly hang-ups over marketing material."

"You probably think Marlboros will turn you into some kind of a wild west cowboy," Fulbright fired back. "But at the end of the day, you're still just smoking a ladies' cigarette."

"Better be careful, or I may not come back with any smokes at all for you," Dex said with a sneer.

Dex took a deep breath as he entered the store. Lost in thought, he meandered down the aisles in a half-hearted search for the cigarette section. The Beatles famed hit "Ticket to Ride" played softly over the loud speakers. A woman pushing a cart with her toddler inside bumped him from behind. Apologizing quickly, she maneuvered past him and headed down the dairy aisle.

Pritchett's words about Voigt still echoed in Dex's mind as he ambled along.

Can we be sure he's not working as a double agent?

Fulbright was emphatic that such a betrayal wasn't possible. But Dex thought his partner should know better given his time working for the agency. Foreign assets were as unpredictable as the weather in Wyoming where Dex grew up. A sunny day could be printed as the forecast in the newspaper, but the torrential downpour outside would render such prognostications useless. When it came to fostering relationships with assets, Dex considered that skill to be one of the sharpest in his arsenal. But even so, he found himself red-faced more times than he cared to admit after an asset changed his mind or tried to turn the tables by running to his government and reporting such meddling.

Replaying in his mind the moment that Voigt made a shifty move to lose them, Dex wondered if he and Fulbright were getting played. The likelihood that they were walking into a trap seemed low, but Dex couldn't ignore his hunch.

He finally located the cigarettes. Grabbing a pack of Marlboros, he snatched some Lucky Strikes too.

"Women's cigarettes," he mumbled to himself as he studied the Marlboros. "Fulbright is a fool in more ways than one."

When Dex exited the store and re-entered the sunlight, he saw Fulbright motioning frantically to hurry up. Dex picked up his pace, hustling toward their vehicle.

Fulbright didn't wait for Dex to get there, sliding into the driver's seat and turning the ignition. The car roared to life and rumbled as it awaited Fulbright to step on the accelerator.

"What is it?" Dex asked as he eased into the passenger's seat.

Fulbright stomped on the gas pedal, forcing Dex back in his seat.

"The homing beacon started working about a minute before you came out of the store," Fulbright said. "I told you CAShadow-5 was trustworthy."

"That doesn't exactly prove anything."

"The hell it doesn't. If he was trying to lose us for good, he would've never turned on his backup. Ivanov probably spotted us or got spooked and made our guy speed out of there. I just knew it."

"You don't get a prize for being right, you know," Dex said.

Fulbright leaned toward Dex. "Can you help me out here?"

Dex shook his head, shoving a Lucky Strike onto Fulbright's lips and then ignited the cigarette.

"Do you know how to use this thing?" Dex asked, staring at the screen with a furrowed brow.

"It's not too complicated. We want to move in the direction of the blinking dot. The closer we get, the louder the beeping will get."

Dex eyed the device carefully. "So, let me get this straight," he said. "I simply help guide you in the general direction of the beeping until it draws closer to the center and then I alert you that we've arrived."

"Something like that," Fulbright said.

He jerked the steering wheel to the right, inertia sending both men leaning in the same direction. Dex hit the side of his door with a thud.

"You all right?" Fulbright asked.

"I would be if you weren't driving like a maniac. The blip isn't moving, which means we don't need to be in a hurry. We can't be more than a couple miles away if this thing is accurate."

"You know it's dead on. Everything Rose creates works to perfection."

"Maybe you should start a Rose Fuller fan club."

"Why are you so punchy today?" Fulbright asked. "I'm just stating a fact."

"Just keep driving. We're almost there."

A couple minutes later, Dex watched the light blink less frequently.

"I think we're here," he said.

"In that run down building right there?" Fulbright said, pointing with his nose in the direction of a new office building.

"Nope," Dex said. "Try the other side of the street."

Fulbright swung around to look in the opposite direction. He noticed the dilapidated structure, which at one time was likely a sparkling jewel of a warehouse. But its better days were far behind it. Rusted-out barrels hugged the outer rim of the building. The charred edges led Dex to believe that at some point in recent history, fires had been built in the cylindrical objects peppering the road that circled the building. A pile of rotting pallets were stacked on one side, while a heap of broken typewriters and corroded pipes sat at the foot of a dumpster.

"You think they're really going to meet here with Zhutov?" Fulbright asked.

Dex shrugged. "Maybe it's a trap."

"No, it's not," Fulbright said as something on the other side of the fence arrested his attention.

"That's their car, isn't it?" Dex asked.

Fulbright nodded slowly. "Still think he isn't trustworthy?"

"The jury is still out."

"How can the jury still be out? He led us to this secret meeting between Ivanov and Zhutov."

"We'd be a nice catch, too, for someone wanting to make an impression with the KGB," Dex said.

"You're so paranoid sometimes."

"Paranoia is what keeps me alive in most situations. And while I trust you, don't think I won't begin to suspect you if some shady things start happening."

"Do I need to remind you that you were the one driving earlier today when we lost CAShadow-5?"

"You're the one driving now," Dex fired back. "Just make sure they don't see us coming."

Fulbright shot Dex a sideways glance. "Can you just trust me here?"

"Fine," Dex said as they both exited the vehicle. "You lead the way."

A chain link fence formed the perimeter around the warehouse. Dex guessed it was at least forty thousand square feet and towered some thirty feet off the ground.

"What did they make in here?" Fulbright whispered over his shoulder.

"I believe they made ball bearings during the war."

Dex looked at the ground and spotted one of the round objects. He stooped down and picked it up. "See," he said. "Looks like I was right."

"And I was right about CAShadow-5 still being on our side. Look over there."

The CIA asset was seated comfortably in the driver's seat of his car, drumming his fingers on the steering wheel. He flashed a quick thumbs up sign, the same one he'd given them while driving around in Bonn traffic. Dex watched a smile flicker across Fulbright's face.

"Scientists say that most betrayals happen with a smile," Dex said.

Fulbright glowered at his partner. "You just hate admitting that I'm right, don't you?"

"Like I said, I'm not convinced."

Fulbright pressed ahead, crouching low and moving along the outer wall toward the door.

Dex kept pace with Fulbright. With specific orders not to engage unless trapped in a gunfight, Dex tried to keep the purpose of this particular operation at the forefront of their minds.

"Why don't we use that side entrance over there," he suggested. "We're only here to listen in. If they figure out we're here, this will all be a big waste of time."

"Do you know the layout of this building?" Fulbright shot back. "What if that doesn't get us where we need to be in order to hear Ivanov and Zhutov discuss their next big plans?"

"Then we'll go in the other entrance."

Fulbright relented and went with Dex's decision, leading them up to the door on the side of the building.

With a slight nod, Fulbright turned the knob and slipped inside. Dex followed, making sure the door didn't slam. The two men froze, listening for the sound of voices.

"Second floor?" Fulbright asked.

Dex nodded in agreement.

They crept up a stairwell and then stopped on the landing. Dex peered through a window in the door to inspect the hallway. Noting the two guards standing outside the room, they decided to go up one more level to find a more optimal place to eavesdrop, a place where they wouldn't be found. Dex pointed up and took the lead.

They entered the third floor and located the room directly over where the guards had been standing. Fulbright pulled out a device that allowed him to listen more clearly to the conversation below them. But Dex could hear everything as they spoke loudly.

After a couple minutes of talking about inane topics, Dex tapped Fulbright on the shoulder.

"What time was this meeting supposed to start?" Dex asked.

"Ten minutes ago. Why?"

"I still haven't heard Zhutov's voice."

Fulbright turned his attention back to the listening device. "Maybe he's running late."

"Zhutov is always on time. And besides, we only saw one car out there."

"So maybe he's stuck in traffic."

"Or maybe he was never intended to be here at all."

"Just keep listening, okay?"

A couple more minutes passed with Ivanov talking to one of his aides about an upcoming dinner meeting. The two men droned on about which restaurant was the best for such gatherings and why.

Then the door swung open and the two guards Dex had seen earlier rushed into the room, weapons drawn.

"Hands in the air," one of the guards said.

Dex and Fulbright both took a posture of surrender, careful to follow orders.

With a sideways glance, Dex asked, "Still think this wasn't a set up?"

VI

DR. HEINRICH SCHWARZ STEPPED back from the chalkboard and studied the equations he had just finished scribbling. Taking a moment to check the numbers, he waited until he was sure they were right before continuing his lecture. He spun around to face his fellow researchers at NASA.

"The Reynolds number needs to be higher," one of the scientists said as he pointed at the board.

"Not necessarily," Schwarz said. "The environment plays a role in how smooth the propulsion can be, but everything changes as the atmospheric conditions change."

"So, you must be suggesting something different, Dr. Schwarz," another scientist chimed in, "because these propulsion engines have failed many times once they exit the earth's atmosphere."

"That's why we need to provide our own oxygen," Schwarz said.

"Are you suggesting that we take tanks of oxygen with us into space?" asked another.

Schwarz nodded. "When it comes to a manned

space flight, we have plenty to still figure out. But for an unmanned rocket launch, I think this approach will work best. Based on what we know about propulsion and the technology we have so far, this seems like the most efficient way."

Schwarz tried to gauge the level of acceptance around the room. From the time he started at NASA, he'd seen plenty of changes, including the renaming of the organization. And if there was one thing he learned, it was that in order to get fellow researchers to buy into the idea, he needed to get a few key influencers excited about a proposal. Otherwise, such suggestions were viewed as little more than science fiction. More importantly, they wouldn't receive a single dime of funding. But if the right people got behind one of Schwarz's ideas, boundaries vanished in terms of how much money he could get from backers anxious to be a part of a major scientific breakthrough.

As Schwarz attempted to get a feel for how the other researchers perceived this suggestion, he was distracted by two men arguing loudly just outside his door. The men shouted at one another at the same time, leaving Schwarz to surmise that there was no productive conversation occurring in the hallway. And the confrontation sounded like it was escalating.

Schwarz couldn't take the disturbance any longer.

"If you'll excuse me for a moment," he said as he stepped into the hall.

He eased outside and closed the door behind him to find two men nearly nose to nose, veins protruding from the necks.

"Would you gentleman mind telling me what's

going on out here?" Schwarz asked. "We're having a serious discussion inside about important research, and all I can hear are the two of you trading barbs. If you must continue this, please go somewhere else."

"If only it were that easy," said the taller man. His Langley security badge clipped to his jacket pocket read John Nielson.

The other man wore a visitor's pass and offered his hand to Schwarz.

"I'm Bill Bankston from the CIA. It's truly an honor to meet you, Dr. Schwarz."

Schwarz scowled. "I still don't understand why you two have been carrying on like you have just outside our room. We're on a tight time schedule and have plenty of scientific ideas to discuss today. These interruptions only pull us away from the important work that we're doing."

"I understand, Dr. Schwarz, but unfortunately this can't wait," Bankston said. "The nature of my business here is urgent and requires immediate action. Unfortunately, Mr. Nielson here isn't being very cooperative."

Neilson glared at Bankston. "That's what happens when you show up unannounced and attempt to rip one of our leading scientists out of this facility without any official accompanying paperwork."

Bankston held up a piece of paper and shook it as he talked. "I showed you this letter straight from the desk of the Director Raborn. I'm not sure what constitutes official paperwork in your world, but any communication directly from the person in charge of our nation's security would satisfy that requirement for most people."

"I'm not most people, and this facility isn't just

some place you can come in and pluck personnel without official transfers," Nielson countered. "Dr. Schwarz is one of our brightest minds and is here at the direct request of the president, who, when I last checked, held a higher rank than Director Raborn. Now, if you don't like it, you can have your boss take it up with the president."

Schwarz threw his hands up in the air and sighed. "Would someone please tell me what's going on here? I really need to get back to my colleagues."

"I'm truly sorry about this interruption," Nielson said. "I'm sure Mr. Bankston and I can work this out and—"

"Agent Bankston—and, no, this isn't something we have to go hash out in your office. This is a direct order, and I'm not about to let you stand in the way."

"What kind of order are you talking about?" asked Schwarz.

Bankston made eye contact with Schwarz. "Two of our agents have been captured by the KGB, and they're demanding that we turn you over to them or else they'll kill the agents."

"This is absurd," Nielson said. "You can't drag him out of here. I'm going to call security."

"I suppose you don't know Dr. Schwarz's background then, do you, Mr. Nielson?"

Nielson shot a quick glance at Schwarz. "Is there something I need to know about one of our best scientists, who's been serving here for nearly a decade?"

"As a matter of fact, there is," Schwarz said as he looked down.

"You don't have to tell him anything," Bankston

said. "Your past is irrelevant at this point. What matters is that we have two high-level intelligence officers who we need to retrieve immediately or risk the KGB extracting information from them—or worse, possibly killing them. We can't afford to lose these two men."

"I don't mind telling Mr. Neilson," Schwarz said. "It might help him understand exactly what's going on."

"Fine," Bankston said. "I'm not stopping you."

"I used to work for the Nazis," Schwarz said. "The CIA tracked me down where I was hiding with my family in Argentina and offered me immunity in exchange for working for the U.S. space program. It was a relief to me. I hated running, and I no longer had to raise my family under the threat of being captured and killed at any moment. Plus, this arrangement has allowed me to continue my work."

"And now the Soviets want you to help them," Nielson said. "The president would most definitely want to hear about this. I doubt he would be so willing to give up one of his precious space program's brightest minds."

Bankston shook his head and forced a laugh. "You'd be surprised what the president would be willing to give up based off what we know about him."

"So, you're blackmailing the president to get this done? Is that what you're telling me?" Nielson asked, his voice escalating.

"All I'm telling you is that those two agents are more valuable than the future of our space program in the grand scheme of things," Bankston said.

An awkward silence fell over the three men, broken after a few seconds by Schwarz.

"Who are the two agents?" Schwarz asked.

"Malcolm Poindexter and Terry Fulbright," Bankston said.

"Terry Fulbright," Schwarz said as he shook his head. "How can I not go? As long as you promise me that my family will be safe and can remain here."

"You have our word," Bankston said.

"Who's Terry Fulbright?" Nielson asked.

"He's the agent who apprehended me in Argentina and brought me to America," Schwarz said. "He could've done whatever he wanted to me and my family, but he showed me mercy when I deserved little. Repaying him by volunteering to be exchanged for his life is the least I can do. Now, if you'll excuse me, I need to inform my colleagues that I will be leaving."

Schwarz returned to the room and shut the door behind him. He leaned against it and took a deep breath.

"What was that all about?" one of the other scientists asked.

"I'm going to be taking a leave of absence," Schwarz said. "I just hope you'll take everything I've shared with you seriously. This is important work."

"You sound like you're not sure if you'll come back," another colleague said.

"I'm not," Schwarz said.

VII

MADDUX OPENED THE DOOR for Rose as they entered the CIA's safe house in Zehlendorf, just a few miles southwest of downtown Berlin. The flat was located on the top floor of a four-story building and had multiple exit points, which he hoped he would never have to utilize. There were two fire escapes, one on each side of the structure, as well as roof access and two stairwells. But the décor inside was what had Rose talking.

The wallpaper consisted of a beige background with pictures of various birds perched on branches jutting out from a floral chain that ran vertically. Situated in the corner of the room was a square wooden table large enough to seat four people comfortably. With scuffs and scrapes on its top and legs, Maddux guessed it was probably built in another era, maybe in another century.

"You don't see furniture made like this any more," Rose said.

"And for good reason," Maddux said. "It's rickety, and I'm not sure I'd trust it to hold a plate of food."

He grabbed the tabletop and wiggled it a little, the legs creaking beneath the stress.

"I see what you mean," she said. "But I have a thing about restoring old furniture and making it look new again."

"Do you feel the same way about tech devices?" he asked as he slung his backpack and briefcase onto the couch in the living room.

She cocked her head to one side and huffed a laugh through her nose. "That's one area where I think the past should remain in the past. Innovation is the key to moving forward, especially in the world of espionage."

Maddux settled into a chair across from the couch. "That's a relief. I'm not sure how long I'd last if I had to do battle with the KGB using ancient technology."

"So you're not that confident in your swords skills?"

"I prefer to do this job without weapons, using them only when absolutely necessary."

She smiled. "In that case, you're going to love this gadget I've been working on for a while. And it'll keep you from getting into a shootout in order to complete your mission."

Maddux hopped up from his chair and then dug through his briefcase until he located the file folder that detailed the operation. After walking over to the kitchen table, he placed the documents down and started sifting through them.

"Speaking of our mission, I want to go over this one more time before I head out to my Opel meeting."

"Very well," she said, easing into a chair at the table. "I'm hoping this goes smoothly."

"It better since I'm going to be on my own for this one."

"I only came because I need to pick up some information on the allied radio network set up in the Soviet bloc. Getting to prep you is just a bonus. I'll be long gone by the time you get back tonight."

Maddux loosened his tie and spread out a map over the table. "Show me where the ideal place to use this device is again. I want to make sure I don't fumble this opportunity."

"No pressure," she said with a wink. "This is a special operation that the president will be monitoring closely."

"I'm less concerned with the initial portion of the mission and more worried about how I'm going to sneak him out. Once we snag him back, the Soviets are going to be crawling all over East Berlin looking for us."

"Good thing they don't know this safe house exists."

Maddux looked at his passport on the table. Instead of entering East Berlin as himself, he was using a legend named Jim Whittaker. While his job with Opel consisted of crisscrossing borders throughout Europe, Pritchett was concerned that too many entries into countries controlled by communist regimes might draw unwanted surveillance. So, Jim Whittaker it was.

Maddux slid a ring onto his finger and fancied the piece of jewelry for a moment.

"You're far less attractive as a married man," Rose said.

Maddux shrugged. "I doubt I'll remain on the market forever. And you might have something to say about that."

"If I didn't know any better, I'd—"

The phone rang, interrupting their banter.

"I better get that," Maddux said as he reached for the receiver.

"Are you sure?" she asked. "Were you expecting anyone to call here?"

"It's probably Pritchett," he said before answering.

"Wait, Ed."

Maddux didn't wait. "Hello."

Silence from the other end.

"Hello," Maddux said again. "Is anyone there?"

Still nothing.

"Hello," Maddux repeated a final time before hanging up.

"Oh great," Rose said. "You probably just alerted the KGB to our position."

"You need to work on some technology that can scramble our conversations so they'd have no idea who we were or what we were saying."

"Good idea, but that doesn't change what you just did."

Maddux waved dismissively. "It's probably nothing to be worried about."

"When I joined the agency, one of my mentors told me a good motto to operate under is 'If you're not worried, you should be.' I'm not sure anyone can be so cocksure in this day and age."

"Okay," Maddux said, "I'll be careful. But that phone call doesn't mean anything. Someone could just be checking to see if we arrived."

"There are plenty of possibilities regarding the nature of that call. All I'm saying is that you need to be on high alert right now. You're about to go behind enemy

lines this afternoon, and I can promise you that the Soviets have the capability to listen to every line in or out
of Berlin—West and East."

Maddux nodded. "I understand. Now, can we get
back to reviewing this operation. I want to make sure
everything runs as planned. If we're going to recover
Dr. Schwarz, we need to be precise about it."

Rose patted Maddux's hand before gripping it
tightly. "Just come back, okay?"

* * *

AN HOUR LATER, Maddux entered East Berlin by
way of the Glienicke Bridge. While there were much
more convenient locations to cross the border, he
wanted to see the scene for the exchange and get a feel
for how things would go down later that evening. The
trade was scheduled to take place at 11:00 p.m., and he
didn't want any surprises.

With his Opel credentials and papers confirming
his meeting that afternoon, he didn't have any issues
with the guards patrolling the entry point on the other
side of the bridge. Maddux even managed to get a faint
smile from one of the men before getting his passport
back.

Heading straight toward the designated extraction
location, he scanned the area for any potential glitches
that could arise as a result of the surrounding environment. Police stations, hospitals, criminal activity—nothing readily appeared to Maddux.

Someone has done their homework.

He pulled into a gas station and studied his map
for a minute.

A station attendant wandered up to Maddux's vehicle.

"Are you lost?" the man asked in German.

"*Nein*," Maddux replied.

The man shrugged and walked away.

Maddux returned to his studying of the area. Having never driven in this section of East Berlin, he decided to make his way along the escape route to ensure that all the streets were working and there were no detours.

After a few minutes, Maddux eased onto the brakes.

"Well, would you look at that?" he said, followed by a drawn-out whistle.

One of the main thoroughfares Maddux was supposed to use was blocked off with a large detour sign. Pulling out the map, he rerouted himself so that he wouldn't even go near the dead end.

Satisfied that he was in good shape for later that evening, he headed straight to his hotel to check in before his meeting. Upon getting settled, he went to the office where he convened with several German officials about the marketing challenges facing Opel in East Germany.

After he finished, he walked back to his hotel, which was two blocks away. The cool air helped him clear his head as he went over all the details about his impending extraction of Dr. Schwarz. Maddux would've preferred a team, but there were two glaring problems with such a wish. For starters, two of the CIA's best agents stationed in Germany were the ones who were being traded. Next, any big operation was suspect to getting thwarted before it ever commenced with secret police swarming around the streets. But Rose assured him that he had all the technology he needed to handle the operation alone.

He stopped and took a deep breath then exhaled slowly. Catching a whiff of freshly brewed coffee from a vendor up ahead on the opposite corner, Maddux crossed the street and purchased a cup. As he was waiting for his drink, he noticed a man take the same route. Maddux fought against the paranoia that began to overtake him, especially after his conversation earlier in the day with Rose. But maybe she was right. Perhaps this wasn't the time to shrug it off. The Soviet influence in this portion of East Berlin was unusually high by all accounts. And to play a hunch that he was being followed wasn't a foolish idea in the least.

Maddux watched as the coffee slowly rose, stopping about three quarters of the way from the top.

"If you'll wait another minute, I have a new pot that will be ready," the vendor said in German.

Maddux reached for the cup, freeing it from the vendor's hands.

"This is plenty," Maddux said before taking a quick sip and then continuing down the sidewalk.

He shot a quick glance over his shoulder and noticed the man was still trailing him. Trying to look casual, Maddux glanced across the street and paused for a moment outside a store, pretending to study what products were displayed in the window.

But Maddux wasn't buying it. Whoever the guy was, he was intent on tracking down Maddux.

Quickening his pace, Maddux darted down an alley off the main road leading to his hotel. If the man didn't know Maddux's lodging destination, revealing it would have been foolish. Maddux resisted the urge to dash behind an object in the first passageway that intersected behind the buildings. During his most recent operation with Dex, Maddux had learned that the farther he traveled before peeling off meant that his pursuer would have to check each one, giving the fleeing person a decisive advantage.

Maddux quickened his pace, bypassing the first and then second turnoffs after tossing his coffee out in the second alley. He opted for the third, which had a large dumpster and several large crates that could be used for cover. After a final glance over his shoulder and no one visible behind him, Maddux cut left and hustled to take cover behind a stack of pallets near the far end of the alley. The decision was a risky one as it would have put him in an impossible situation if the man caught up. But Maddux trusted Dex, who also told him that most pursuers won't go all the way down an alley to check for fear that they might get ambushed. Maddux didn't have a gun on him since he was returning from his business meeting, though he considered how he might weaponize his briefcase. But even that was a long shot. All he could do was hope that Dex was right.

Maddux crouched low and swallowed hard as he heard footsteps approaching. The man was systematically working his way down the alley, turning over every stack of crates and pallets. The mix of the shadows and the dusky sky overhead made it difficult for Maddux to make out the man's face.

But Maddux could see enough to tell that the man wasn't slowing down and seemed intent on overturning every obstacle the lined the back steps of the adjacent businesses and apartment buildings. Maddux felt his mouth getting dry.

He clutched the handle on his briefcase, his hands beading up with sweat. Unarmed in a dark alley wasn't an optimal situation for Maddux, but it was the hand he'd been dealt. The attaché case would have to suffice.

Hunched over, he recoiled and prepared to spring. The man was close enough that the smell of his cologne and his heavy breathing assaulted Maddux's senses.

It was only a matter of seconds before a melee ensued.

PRITCHETT SAT IN THE BOOTH across from Dr. Schwarz and stared at the piece of apple pie the waitress had just placed on the table. The steam was still rising from the top, and the sweet smell had already wafted to Pritchett's nose. Immediately, he called the waitress back over to the table to order a piece for himself.

Schwarz's eyes lit up as he pulled the dessert closer to his side of the table. He wasted no time in digging in.

Pritchett shifted in his seat as his mouth watered.

"Of all the things you claim you're going to miss about living in America, I never would've guessed that apple pie would be near the top of the list," he said.

"This doesn't compare to apple strudel, which is all I'll be able to get if anything wherever the Russians take me."

"We know where they're planning to take you," Pritchett said.

"Well, don't keep me in suspense," Schwarz said, scooping up another piece of the pie with his fork.

"Kaliningrad, just northeast of Moscow. It's where the main research facility for the Soviet Union's space program is located."

"Sounds delightful," Schwarz said, his reply dripping with sarcasm.

"However, I doubt you'll ever make it there."

Schwarz put down his fork and dabbed the corners of his mouth with a napkin. "Do you think they're going to kill me? Because it seems like they're going to a lot of trouble to do so, giving up a pair of U.S. spies."

"No, but we intend to get you back before you get very far."

"And how are you going to do that?"

The waitress returned with Pritchett's pie and slid it onto the table in front of him. He didn't answer until he had gobbled up a piece.

"We already have people on the other side who will break you out before you can leave East Berlin."

"And you think this plan is going to work?"

"Nothing is ever certain when it comes to these types of operations, but I wanted to let you know that we are going to do everything in our power to make sure that you don't end up in Kaliningrad. The fact that you've been willing to do this has impressed several people at the agency who fully expected that we'd be dragging you away."

"I've been dragged away before, and it's not very pleasant. Besides, the CIA could've killed me a long time ago for my affiliation with the Nazis. But like my dealings with the American space program, I didn't have much of a choice. Fortunately, the Americans have been far kinder than any other nation would've been who found me, even if I am being used for my scientific knowledge and expertise."

"The research you're doing for the Americans is

going to benefit the world not just a tyrannical regime. Do you really think the Nazis or the Soviets would share what they learn in space with everyone else? The answer is no. They would use it to dominate those around them. The Soviets have already rushed satellites into orbit and are using them to spy on us. Just think what they might do if they start putting manned aircraft into space."

"At this point, that is all speculation, though I understand why you're concerned. Pardon me if I sound jaded, but I have very little faith in any government organization, no matter the country. I've found them all to be self-serving on some level, if not completely so. Even if our team at Langley had managed to uncover a way to propel a manned aircraft into space, I doubt we would've shared our findings with everyone else."

"Perhaps not, but the American government certainly wouldn't use it to run roughshod over neighboring countries and try to dominate the world. I can assure you that our ultimate intentions are good."

Schwarz finished his piece of pie. "Mr. Pritchett, you tell yourself whatever you need to tell yourself to feel better about what you're doing. At this point, I've simply accepted my fate as a passenger on this planet. I'd prefer to stay in America with my family, but if not I'll live with the consequences of my actions, even though they were never of my own volition."

"And I'm telling you that we're doing everything we can to make sure you get your preferred living situation," Pritchett said. "When President Johnson weighs in on a situation like this, you know that we're damn sure going to do our best to get you back as soon as possible."

Schwarz pushed his plate toward the side of the table. "I appreciate the sentiments and the effort on your part. And if your team is successful in getting me home, I'll be grateful. Yet I wonder what's to stop this proposed exchange from being attempted again."

"Nothing guarantees that the Russians won't try again, except maybe you helping the Americans win the race to space. If we get there first, we'll mitigate any type of intimidation tactics they plan to use on the rest of the world. Putting people in space, and, more importantly, a man on the moon, will give us and everyone else a peace of mind."

"Let's hope I get the opportunity to do that," Schwarz said. "I feel like we're getting closer and it's just a matter of time."

Pritchett glanced at his watch. "And time is a commodity that we're short of at the moment. We need to get going or we're going to be late."

* * *

AT FIVE MINUTES before eleven, Pritchett stood outside in the guardhouse on the eastern side of the Glienicke Bridge. He eyed Schwarz to make sure he wasn't getting cold feet and would do something rash. With a swift current that wouldn't overwhelm a decent swimmer, the Havel River below could easily sustain a leap from a height of twenty feet. And under the shroud of night, a determined person might be able to escape to safety.

Pritchett could only hope that Schwarz wasn't playing him. Losing Fulbright and Dex would be a major blow to the agency's efforts at counterintelligence in Bonn. But that was already a foregone conclusion given that their capture would facilitate them transferring to a different station. Spies with blown covers were no longer useful in the field.

"Are you sure you want to follow through with this?" Pritchett asked Schwarz.

"At this point, do I really have a choice?"

"Guess you're ready," Pritchett said with a shrug. "Now, I'll signal you when it's time to cross the bridge. You will walk at a slow pace to the other side, passing our two agents near the midway point. Don't make any sudden movements or start running. The last thing we want is for some trigger-happy soldier to get suspicious about anything you're doing. And I doubt you want to get caught in the crossfire either."

"I'd like to avoid that at all costs," Schwarz said.

"Excellent. So, just keep a steady pace and put your hands where they can be visible to the Russians and you should be fine."

"The KGB is not going to shoot me. I'm more valuable to them alive than I am dead. If I'm dead, I'm just not working with the Americans. But if I'm alive, I can help them achieve their goals of reaching space. I'm sure they're under strict orders not to shoot me."

"Just don't get cute, okay?" Pritchett said. "Stick to the plan. If we both play our parts in this operation, we'll have you back home with your family within a week at the most, probably less."

Pritchett briefed the Army guards standing watch one final time, reminding them of how they would receive Fulbright and Dex.

"Under no circumstances are you to fire your weapon while the prisoners are being exchanged on the bridge," Pritchett said. "We need everything to go smoothly. And just know that the president is personally interested in the outcome of this trade."

The commanding officer nodded knowingly.

"We've done this before, sir," he said. "You're in the best hands possible for this prisoner swap. We can sense if something is amiss."

Pritchett patted the officer on the back and wished him luck. Meandering back to Schwarz, Pritchett studied the physicist one more time before saying a quick prayer beneath his breath. While lives were at stake along with plenty of state secrets, Pritchett felt the magnitude of the situation flood over like a tidal wave battering the shore. He valued Fulbright and Dex as not only as assets to use in the field but also as people. They were friends who'd been through shared experiences within the agency. They were friends who'd become family.

And then there was the underlying thought Pritchett couldn't shake: his job was on the line. With President Johnson so invested in the space program and Schwarz being heralded as the brightest mind who could help the U.S. win the space race, Pritchett sensed that this moment could be a crossroads of sorts for his career. If he succeeded in getting Schwarz back, Pritchett could possibly name his position. If he failed, he suspected he'd be buried somewhere in Washington, pushing paper until he retired, though he would consider that a generous assignment.

Pritchett watched the second hand on his watch sweep past the top as both hands moved into the eleven o'clock position.

"Time to go," Pritchett said. "Just remember what we told you."

Schwarz nodded without saying a word and embarked on his steady walk along the bridge. Across the way, the shadowy figures of two men plodded toward the American side.

Pulling out his binoculars to get a closer look, Pritchett peered through his one good eye and verified that Fulbright and Dex were the men heading toward them. Adjusting the focus, Pritchett turned his attention to the Russian guards, several of which had their guns trained in a forward position.

"Why are they pointing their weapons toward us?" Pritchett asked the commanding officer.

"Take it easy, Chief. That's just their standard procedure. They know better than to open fire."

"But what if they do?"

"Then we'll respond with the appropriate countermeasures. Just relax."

How am I supposed to relax? I'll relax when everyone makes it alive to the side of the bridge they're supposed to be on.

Quick, shallow breaths resulted in Pritchett starting to feel lightheaded.

"They're almost here, Chief," the officer said, patting Pritchett on the back.

He looked up and saw Dex and Fulbright less than twenty meters away.

Come on. You can do it.

Each step seemed to take place in slow motion, each stride shorter than it could be. Pritchett held his breath as they approached.

Dex shook Pritchett's hand first before giving him a hug. Fulbright went straight for a hug. Both men wasted no time in expressing their gratitude.

"Let's get out of here," Pritchett said.

Dex stopped. "Who was that the Russians just traded us for?"

"Dr. Heinrich Schwarz, one of the most brilliant physicists in the world," Pritchett said. "But don't worry, he's not going to remain in their possession for long."

"And why is that?"

"Maddux is going to free him for us, and we're going to smuggle him back across the border."

"Who else is with Maddux?" Fulbright asked.

"He's on his own this time," Pritchett said.

Dex shook his head.

"Then you just sent him to his death. They transport prisoners with a slew of guards. It'd be impossible for both of them to escape without getting killed. You need to abort if you want to see Maddux alive again."

Pritchett sighed. "There's nothing I can do now. The operation takes place within the hour, and there's no way to contact him now. Let's get moving."

After ushering Dex and Fulbright to the car, Pritchett paused before getting inside and looked skyward at the pale moon. He said another quick prayer, this time for Maddux.

MADDUX COULD FEEL his heart pounding in his chest as the scuffling of footsteps drew nearer. For a moment, he wondered if the man a few meters away could hear the thumping too.

After he flipped over a nearby pile of pallets, Maddux debated between a surprise attack and praying that the man wouldn't see him.

A shrill whistle made Maddux pause.

At the intersecting passageway, another man shouted something in German. Maddux watched as his pursuer spun around and sprinted back toward the alley entrance, banking right and turning in the direction he came from.

For more than a minute, Maddux hardly breathed, unsure if what he saw was a tactic to draw him out. Glancing down at his watch, he realized he couldn't stay there any longer. His window of opportunity for snatching Dr. Schwarz back from the Russians was going to vanish if he didn't hurry.

Maddux eased out from his hiding spot and raced toward his hotel, which was less than a block away. He entered the parking lot and hustled toward his car. After opening the door, he slid behind the wheel and tossed his briefcase into the backseat. He turned the ignition key, and the car rumbled to life.

Maddux gunned the engine and sped toward the rendezvous point. As he drove, various thoughts danced through his mind. He went over the new route to prevent him from getting stuck in a detour. Then he reviewed the steps for turning on the device Rose had given him. She also had given him a gas mask and two canisters that would knock out everyone in a ten-meter radius.

"One for the drivers, and one for the guards," she'd told him.

Maddux inquired about Schwarz's size, knowing that lugging him into the car was a likely scenario. At five foot seven and thin, she had assured Maddux that the task of carrying Schwarz wouldn't be all that difficult.

Maddux drove along the assigned route, one CIA contacts had observed KGB transports taking when leaving the Glienicke Bridge in the past. His watch showed just two minutes past eleven, which meant he'd have about five minutes to get set up. After slowing down a few hundred meters around a bend that sloped upward, Maddux came to a stop with half of his vehicle still in the road. He got out and went to work, setting up the device that was cleverly hidden inside a hollowed-out compartment in the engine. Rose's ingenuity in getting the device in his car was vital since the large electronic apparatus would likely be confiscated at any border crossing.

Maddux set up the gadget up, connecting it to his car's battery after popping the hood. All there was left to do now was wait. The clouds drifted across the sky, hiding the pale moon for large swaths of time before the light reemerged. He leaned against the back of the trunk, peering around the corner for the distinct yellow lights that lined the top of the transport truck's cab. But Maddux didn't need to see the lights, hearing the roaring engine from afar first as it strained to get up the hill.

Maddux activated the device, which pulsed strongly and was designed to kill any engine motors that were currently operating. As the truck neared him, it suddenly died and the wheels locked up as the vehicle skidded to a stop a few meters short of Maddux's car. He casually walked toward the truck, carrying the mask in one hand and a canister in the other.

The driver was about to step down when Maddux hustled up to him.

"Are you having engine problems, too?" Maddux asked in German.

Before the man could respond, Maddux secured the mask on his face and pulled the plug on the can, unleashing the gas. After a few seconds of coughing and wheezing, the driver and the guard riding in the passenger's seat collapsed on the bench in the cab. Maddux grabbed the guard's gun and hustled around to the back.

After pulling the other container out of his pocket, Maddux pounded on the door. One of the guards unlatched the lock and poked his head out.

"What's going on?" he asked in German.

Maddux, who was standing around the side of the van, darted forward and tossed the canister inside before surprising the guard and slamming the door into his head. The guard toppled backward into the holding compartment. Without hesitating, Maddux put his shoulder into the door and rammed it shut. He held his body against it and waited for the men to stop attempting to escape.

But they didn't. More than thirty seconds passed before Maddux realized the gas wasn't working. Backing away from the door, Maddux drew his newfound weapon and prepared for a fight.

The guard who'd initially poked his head out careened against the door, flinging it wide open as he tumbled to the ground. Maddux ran up to the guard and kicked him in the face. The guard tried to fight back but was quickly subdued after a pair of powerful punches to his head.

Within seconds, the other guard barreled outside with his gun firing. Maddux scrambled to take cover, seeking a more advantageous spot to engage the man in a gunfight. The guard unleashed a flurry of shots into the dark, emptying his weapon. From the shadows, Maddux watched the man try to reload his gun.

Maddux seized his opportunity to conquer the guard without killing him. Pritchett didn't want to explain any dead bodies to CIA brass unless it was absolutely necessary. And while Maddux could've gotten away with shooting the Soviet guard, there were other options available. Before the guard could see what was coming, Maddux stormed toward the man, bowling him over. They wrestled on the ground for a moment before Maddux took a power position.

"Get up," Maddux said, training his gun on the

man. "I'd rather not kill you."

The guard sneered and spit at Maddux.

"Shoot me," the guard said with a broken English accent. "Are you afraid to do it, you gutless American?"

The guard made a quick move toward Maddux, and he squeezed the trigger, but nothing happened. The gun had jammed. Continuing his momentum toward Maddux, the guard put his head down and drove Maddux backward. They rolled around on the ground for a few more seconds, trading punches before the guard escaped and raced back toward the truck.

Maddux scrambled after him, nearly grabbing the guard by his belt several times. But Maddux's hand kept slipping. With the guard hustling inside, he unlocked a small metal box and began digging through it. Maddux delivered a wicked hit from behind, forcing the man forward as he hit his head on the truck's metal siding.

As Maddux recoiled to deliver another punch, out of the corner of his eye, he noticed Schwarz wink. Maddux glanced down to see Schwarz slide his legs out as far as he could reach them, placing them directly behind the guard. Catching on, Maddux put his head down and raced toward the man.

Upon impact, the guard stumbled backward before taking a hard spill. Schwarz's legs had tripped up the man, ending with a skull-cracking crash into the side of the truck. Maddux delivered one more punch, knocking the man out.

"You made it," Schwarz said, his eyes dancing with delight. "I didn't really expect it was going to happen."

Maddux ripped the keys off the guard and unlocked Schwarz.

"Well, we're not out of the woods yet. We need to hurry before they all wake up."

Maddux worked quickly to free Schwarz. The two men teamed up to handcuff the guards in the back to one of the overhead bars and fasten the two men in the front to the steering wheel. Before leaving, Maddux lifted a gun off the guard in the front. Then Maddux took the guard's knife and jammed it into the front left tire of the truck.

"That ought to give us enough of a head start," Maddux said as he led Schwarz to the car.

Maddux made his official introduction as he fired up his car and whipped it around to travel in the direction from which he originally came.

"Pleased to make your acquaintance," Schwarz said. "I'm Dr. Heinrich Schwarz, and I appreciate your efforts to free me."

"Just doing my job, Doc," Maddux said as they bumped along the two-lane road.

"Mind if I smoke?" Schwarz asked, eyeing the pack of Lucky Strikes and lighter on the dashboard.

"Help yourself."

Schwarz packed down the cigarettes before tapping one out. He fiddled with the lighter for a few seconds before igniting the tobacco. "So, what's the plan now?"

"I have to wait for orders," Maddux said. "What happened back there—it wasn't supposed to go down like that. They were never supposed to see my face. You wouldn't have even seen my face until you woke up in my hotel room if things had gone as planned."

Schwarz chuckled. "It's called life. Nothing ever goes how you planned it."

"It sure would be nice if it did."

"You got that right," Schwarz said, flicking some ashes out his window. "I can promise you that I never planned to apply what I learned to the most ruthless regime the world has seen in several centuries only to live in hiding in South America before being handed my freedom in exchange for working for the American government. Certainly not how I saw my life on this planet going. But I've learned you just have to pick up the pieces and move on."

Maddux nodded and sighed. He turned to say something to Schwarz but never got a chance.

He couldn't even scream the words "Look out!" before a truck broadsided them.

PRITCHETT TAPPED HIS FOOT nervously on the floor as he awaited Dex and Fulbright to arrive at the CIA's West Berlin station to administer their debriefing. With a phone call with CIA brass slated for later that day, Pritchett wanted to be able to tell them something noteworthy. Even if it was just a simple report about how his agents didn't give up any information, that would suffice. He just needed anything to stave off the inevitable question that he had no answer to at the moment: Where was Dr. Heinrich Schwarz?

Maddux was supposed to check in with Pritchett once Schwarz was secure. Worried that Maddux might call the office in Bonn, Pritchett assigned one of his agents to stay at the office all night and answer the phones. Pritchett retreated to the safe house in West Berlin with Dex and Fulbright before falling asleep while watching the phone and praying it would ring.

Pritchett awoke to a loud ringing from the agent who'd remained behind. The report had disappointed and worried Pritchett: Maddux had yet to check in.

At the CIA's West Berlin station, a few short

blocks from the safe house, Pritchett had taken over one of the vacant offices. He checked his watch. Dex and Fulbright were late and had yet to notify him about any delays. Pritchett stood and began pacing around the office. After circling the room several times, he stopped near the window and glanced down at the street below. Perched seven floors above the ground, Pritchett could still identify Dex's trademark strut.

Finally.

Pritchett sighed before settling into his chair and scanning a few briefings.

At least we got our men back last night.

When Dex and Fulbright finally reached the office, the former knocked softly on the doorjamb. Pritchett waved them in and invited them to sit down across from him.

"I know you two weren't ready to talk last night, but what about now?" Pritchett began. "I'm glad you're home, but Washington wants some answers real soon, and I'd love to be able to give them some."

"We were set up," Dex said with a sneer.

"I think that much is obvious," Pritchett said. "Are you sure about who did this to you?"

"CAShadow-5," Fulbright said matter-of-factly. "No doubt about it. It was an elaborate set up just to ambush us."

Pritchett nodded. "And it was all about getting Dr. Schwarz."

Fulbright dropped his head and looked at his shoes.

"He probably only came because they mentioned my name, right?" he asked.

"That's how I understand things went down," Pritchett said.

"Dammit," Fulbright said, pounding his fist onto the desk. "I should've seen it coming."

"The ambush and betrayal or the way they got to Dr. Schwarz?" Pritchett asked.

"All of it," Fulbright said. "Damn good spy craft by the KGB, but we should've been better."

"It's not over yet," Pritchett said. "We still have a chance to come out on top in the end."

"In the end?" Dex asked. "Does that mean you've heard from Maddux?"

"Not yet."

Dex leaned forward in his chair. "Then we need to look for him."

"You're not going anywhere," Pritchett said. "After we debrief here, I'm sending you back to Bonn. There's no way you'd be able to help us in East Berlin anyway after getting captured. Moving you in and out of the country will be next to impossible in the foreseeable future."

Fulbright crossed his arms and slumped deeper in his chair.

"That makes all of this even worse. We're gonna be on desk duty, aren't we?"

Pritchett nodded. "At least until things die down and we can find a way to get you back in the field. Just be thankful you're not still sitting in the custody of the Soviets while they make plans to send you to Siberia. I promise you that it could be worse—much worse."

Pritchett adjusted his eye patch and stood. He paced around the room for a moment before stopping behind his desk and leaning forward on the back of his chair. "So, either one of you want to tell me what happened while you were being held? Did they treat you like animals? Torture you? Try to squeeze secrets out of you?"

Dex shrugged. "If they tortured us, it was with kindness. They fed us three hot meals a day and never shackled us unless we were being transported. I knew they were planning on trading us for someone they wanted. I just never would've guessed it was for a scientist."

"Same experience for you, Fulbright?"

"We were together the whole time. I fully expected them to push us to the brink in order to get some actionable intel, but they didn't even try. It's like they didn't think we were worth the time."

"Or they didn't have the time," Pritchett said. "I'm sure they knew how valuable you two were, but it appears that you served a great purpose to them—pawns in the game to get one of the world's greatest physicists that hardly anyone knows about."

Fulbright shook his head. "Obviously, the Russians knew about him, which means we have a leak somewhere back home."

"Tell me something I don't already know," Pritchett said. "Anything else I can tell the folks in Washington?"

"I overheard some chatter about an upcoming operation they were planning," Dex said. "I think they called it 'Storm,' but I could be wrong."

"Any details you learned?"

"Not sure exactly, but from what I could gather, it sounded like they have agents living in America already who will be ready to take action on a moment's notice."

"Well, that's not a surprise, but it's something," Pritchett said.

"What else do you need from us, sir?" Fulbright asked.

"There's a train at 2:30 this afternoon that will take you back to Bonn," Pritchett said. "I'll be following you later this evening. I'm hoping to make contact with Maddux before I leave, but I'm heading back either way. The station here can handle whatever else might arise with him in my absence and take care of getting Maddux and Schwarz back—if they made it back alive."

"Thank you, sir," Dex said. "We'll look forward to speaking with you tomorrow—and putting down CAShadow-5 at our first opportunity."

Pritchett wagged his index finger. "Let's not be so hasty to eliminate him. He might be useful to us yet."

With the wave of his hand, Pritchett dismissed them. He watched the pair of agents leave before he glanced up at the clock on the far wall. In less than two minutes, the phone would ring and he'd be on the line with some of the CIA's top decision makers, including Director Raborn.

Pritchett straightened piles of paper scattered on his desk before jotting down a few notes from his conversation with Dex and Fulbright.

One of the secretaries breezed into Pritchett's office and handed him a letter with his name on the outside of the envelope. She was perky and cute. Pritchett wanted to wink at her, but he had long since come to grips with the fact that any wink he attempted with his patch on merely appeared as if he was blinking. He thanked her and smiled.

Once she disappeared down the hallway, his phone rang.

"Pritchett," he said as he answered.

"I have Director Raborn for you on a secure line," said one of the secretaries. "Please hold."

After a few clicks, Raborn's nasally voice came through unusually clear.

"I know you are a busy man, as am I," Raborn said, "so I'm sure you don't mind that we dispense with the pleasantries and get straight to business."

"Yes, sir," Pritchett said.

"I have a few other officials in the room with me, including a couple of men working with the space program. We're all anxious to hear about how last night's operation went."

"In terms of retrieving our agents, it was a resounding success," Pritchett said. "Both Agents Poindexter and Fulbright have been returned unharmed to us. In fact, I just debriefed both men, and they made it clear that they didn't divulge any secrets. And oddly enough, they weren't even asked to."

"Sounds like the ambush to seize our two agents was exactly what we thought it was about—getting back Dr. Schwarz," Raborn said.

"It would certainly appear that way, sir. Both agents told me they were treated well and respectfully."

"And what about Dr. Schwarz? Were you able to recover him?"

"I wish I could give you a more definitive answer, sir, but at the moment I'm unable to."

"What seems to be the problem?"

Pritchett took a deep breath, exhaling slowly before answering. "I've yet to hear from Agent Maddux about how his operation went last night."

The silence from the other end extended longer than Pritchett would've hoped for. As it dragged on, he wondered if Raborn was still on the line.

"Sir?" Pritchett said.

"We're all still here," Raborn answered. "And we're all trying to figure out what your answer means."

"I wish I could tell you more regarding their status, but Maddux hasn't checked in yet."

"Is this typical behavior for him?" Raborn asked.

"No, but—"

"From what I understand, Agent Maddux is still relatively new. Why didn't you coordinate with the station in East Berlin and have one of their more seasoned agents handle this?"

"The exchange was to take place leading into a district that is completely controlled by the Soviets. The other agents stationed in East Berlin would've drawn immediate suspicion and assigned a tail from the KGB. We needed someone who could get in and out without attracting too much attention. And Maddux may be green, but he's proven himself time and time again. I have full confidence in his skills."

"I hope that confidence translates into a successful mission for your sake," Raborn said.

Pritchett hesitated before responding, understanding the implications of the director's last statement, then doubling down on his faith in Maddux.

"Maddux will get Schwarz home, sir, one way or another."

"He better. The president is breathing down my neck to get Schwarz back to working with the space program. Giving up Schwarz wasn't something the president wanted to let us do, but I assured him that you'd be able to pull this off. Don't make me look like a fool."

"You won't."

"Good. I want an update in twelve hours, even if you still haven't heard from Maddux."

"I'll call you by that time, if not sooner. The moment we hear from Maddux, I'll contact you."

Raborn hung up, and Pritchett sighed. He couldn't be sure of anything, much less that Maddux was going to succeed. Without a shred of information about what went down the previous night, Maddux could already be dead in a shallow grave and Schwarz on his way to Moscow.

Pritchett didn't even have a chance to tell Raborn about the intel gleaned by Dex and Fulbright while in custody of the Russians. It was obvious the only thing Raborn cared about was completely out of Pritchett's control.

MADDUX'S CAR SPUN around twice before coming to a stop in the middle of the road. The truck that hit Maddux and Schwarz collided with the back third of their vehicle between the trunk and the back seat. If the truck had struck them closer to the front, the likelihood of survival would've been low.

As soon as their car started spinning, Maddux's instinct was to slam on the brakes. That reaction did nothing to stop them. With inertia wreaking havoc on them, Maddux's head smacked against the glass and shattered it. Schwarz managed to maintain consciousness and avoid serious injury by covering his head with his arms. When the spinning stopped, he had several cuts and bruises but nothing to keep him from springing into action to help save Maddux.

Unsure if the crash was intentional or accidental, Schwarz grabbed the gun Maddux had placed in the glove box. After unbuckling him, Schwarz tried to get out but couldn't get the door open. He looked outside and saw the other driver staggering toward them with some object in his hand.

Schwarz scrambled across the front seat and climbed over Maddux to get out. Once Schwarz reached the road, he shoved the gun in the back of his pants before looking up to see the other man clutching a liquor bottle and cursing in German.

"Can you help my friend?" Schwarz asked in German as he gestured toward Maddux.

The man sneered and laughed. "You ran a stop sign, and now my truck is ruined. Now I'm going to make you pay."

Schwarz backpedaled, moving toward the front of the car. He put his hands up in a gesture of surrender. "I promise we will make it right, but my friend needs help right now."

"I don't care about your friend. He's the one who got in my way."

Schwarz glanced at the intersection and noticed that there was no stop sign in the direction Maddux had been traveling. But there was one posted alongside the road where the driver had failed to stop.

The sound of breaking glass arrested Schwarz's attention. He looked back at the man to see he'd taken the liquor bottle and bashed it against the pavement, leaving him with a jagged weapon. The man continued to walk toward Schwarz, who resumed his retreat backward.

"That's far enough," Schwarz said. "This doesn't have to get out of hand."

The man grinned but didn't stop.

Schwarz whipped out his gun, using both hands to train the weapon on his aggressor. "I said *that's far enough.*"

The man finally stopped and dropped what was left

of his bottle before it shattered on the ground. Then he reached behind his back and produced a gun, creating a tense standoff.

"I'm going to get what is due to me," the man said with a growl. "You don't look like the kind of man who has shot many guns in your life. But I can promise you that I have."

"You served in the *Wehrmacht*?"

The man nodded. "At Chelmno. I oversaw the extermination of those—"

He dropped his gun and grasped at his neck as blood spewed out. Tumbling to the ground, he screamed in agony. But it didn't last long before he was dead.

Clutching a piece of bloodied glass, Maddux stood over the man. "Damn Nazi was about to start bragging about killing innocent people."

Schwarz exhaled and jumped to his feet. "Are you okay?"

Maddux squinted and grabbed his head with both hands. After a few seconds, he gave a faint nod. "What just happened?"

"You just killed a man."

"I was talking about before that."

"He ran a stop sign and hit us from the side. I guess it knocked you out. Then you decided to murder this guy."

"I prefer the term *eliminated*," Maddux said. "Besides, you worked with the Nazis. You think a drunk former guard who oversaw a death camp was going to think twice about killing you?"

"You're probably right."

"I saw him waving his gun at you and heard what

he said. I figured there was no reason to waste time dealing with the morality of my actions if it meant you were going to end up dead. I have a mission right now, and that's to get you back home safely."

"Thanks," Schwarz said as he looked around. "We've got quite a mess to clean up now. And we need to hurry before someone comes along and sees us."

Maddux nodded toward the man's truck. "You think that thing still runs?"

"There's only one way to find out. And I'll let you do the honors."

Maddux hustled over to the vehicle and found the keys still in the ignition. As he turned the key, the engine roared to life. He left the truck running before hopping out and sharing his plan with Schwarz. They worked quickly, dragging the body into a ditch and covering the stiff with limbs and leaves. Next, they pushed their car into an opening in the woods, far enough away from the road that no one would notice. Maddux switched the license plates and then hustled back to the truck.

"Now what?" Schwarz asked.

"We need to ditch this truck soon, but I need to get you to one of our safe houses so someone can extract you."

Schwarz's eyes widened. "You're going to leave me in East Berlin?"

"That car was specially designed to sneak you over the border and out of the country. Every Soviet guard in the city is going to be looking for you now—and me, too. We're going to have to come up with another plan, one that doesn't involve us sneaking out together."

Maddux drove them back to a more populated

area and parked the truck a couple blocks from the safe house he learned about just in case of an emergency such as this. Before, the street was virtually empty and quiet with the exception of an occasional barking dog or car engine whining in the distance. The sparsely lit street provided a good cover for the two men but also shrouded anyone else potentially watching the location.

Leading the way up the steps, Maddux wrapped his hand around the gun stuffed in the back of his pants, ready to draw in the event that he encountered any KGB or Soviet guards scouring the area looking for them.

When Maddux arrived at the top of the landing, he noticed the door to the safe house was ajar. He put his index finger to his lips as he turned to look at Schwarz. Maddux softly pushed the door open and slipped inside. He found a pair of CIA agents dead, one on the couch and one in the chair across from him. Both of them had been shot close range, likely surprised by their attackers.

Maddux gestured for Schwarz to turn around and leave. They both crept quietly down the stairs and back to the street level.

"Now what?" Schwarz asked. "Should we check into a hotel?"

Maddux shook his head. "They'll be checking every one of those in the area. But there is one more safe house a few blocks from here, one that Pritchett told me he set up. The East Berlin station chief even knows about it. Guess that was Pritchett's way of always having a fallback in case things got too sketchy within the agency. If Pritchett's site is still secure, we know which station has been compromised."

"I don't care about all that," Schwarz said. "Just keep me safe and get me home."

"I'll do the best I can."

Maddux doubled back and retraced their steps, moving in large sweeping circular routes until he was certain no one was tailing them. Taking Schwarz inside an apartment building and up a narrow stairwell, Maddux finally reached the safe house Pritchett had described. The place was still locked, which Maddux took as a good sign. He jimmied the lock open and eased inside.

"*Hallo*," Maddux said.

No response. He tried again.

"*Ist hier jemand?*" he called.

Nothing.

Maddux secured the door. He went over to the fridge and opened it. Fresh food was packed inside.

"Looks like someone was just here. Maybe Pritchett thought we might need to use this place. You should be able to stay holed up here for a while."

"You're really going to leave me here by myself, aren't you?"

"We don't have a choice if we both hope to get back across the border. Now, let's get some sleep, and we'll sort things out in the morning."

* * *

THE NEXT MORNING, Maddux arose at 5:30, long before the sun even peeked over the horizon. With the border opening up at 6:00 a.m., he wanted to get back to West Berlin before the news of Schwarz's escape spread.

Maddux showered and made a quick breakfast of

eggs and toast along with a pot of coffee that stirred Schwarz's senses. He stumbled into the kitchen, rubbing his eyes.

"I'm pretty sure I could get used to rooming with a chef," he said before inhaling the aroma wafting through the room.

"Unfortunately, this is just a one-time occurrence," Maddux said. "I need to get going."

"Get going?" Schwarz said, his eyes widening. "We haven't even talked about the next steps."

Maddux took a sip of his coffee. "The plan was simple once I broke you out. I was going to use a specially built compartment in the back of my car to smuggle you across the line. But that drunk Nazi ruined that idea. So, we'll need to go in another direction."

"And what exactly does that look like?"

"I'll send some people by to get you out of here in the next couple of days."

"How will I know the people who come to help me are with the CIA?"

"Write down a code phrase," Maddux said, reaching for a pad on the kitchen counter. He rooted through one of the drawers and found a pencil.

Schwarz scribbled down the words "rockets to nowhere" and handed it back to Maddux. He pulled out his lighter and burned the note over the sink. Washing the ashes down the drain, he cast a quick glance at Schwarz.

"That's an interesting choice," Maddux said.

"It's a science fiction book I read with one of my daughters. If I ever get back to America, I might be able to make it come partially true."

"We'll do our best, and I hope we don't let you down."

Schwarz thanked Maddux and grabbed him just as he was leaving.

"Can I use this phone?"

"No, not under any circumstances," Maddux said. "Any contact you get from us will be made in person. I don't trust this place, even though it hasn't been compromised yet."

"Okay," Schwarz said as he shook Maddux's hand. "Thanks for everything."

"Don't thank me yet," Maddux said before he shut the door behind him and hustled down the steps.

He considered finding a payphone first and calling Pritchett, but with the likelihood that Schwarz's escape had already spread, there would be a heightened listening campaign over the phone lines. And with Soviet guards combing the area in search of the pair, separating was the best idea to avoid suspicion.

Maddux drove to the nearest border crossing location and took his place in line. There were several produce trucks on each side, waiting to cross over. The guards snuck cash into the hands of the drivers, hoping to receive rare goods from the west. Watching the exchange, Maddux shook his head in disbelief. A shared culture had been rent in two, and the separation was painful, one that neither side really wanted to let go of. When it was united, Berlin was at its best. Instead, it had just become a broken city, a constant reminder of how war not only ravages physical structures but also the souls of those left to pick up the pieces.

The brake lights of the vehicle in front of Maddux

blinked off as it moved ahead. Easing the truck forward, Maddux rolled down his window and handed his passport to the guard holding out a gloved hand.

"Papers please," he said, even though Maddux had beat him to it.

The guard opened the document and studied Maddux's picture. "Jim Whittaker," the guard announced, continuing in English. "What kind of business were you on during your stay here in East Berlin?"

"I had a meeting at Opel."

The guard continued to look at the passport as he nodded. "You're in the automobile industry?"

"Yes, sir."

"Well, that's interesting. I don't know too many people who work at Opel and drive another type of vehicle."

Maddux reminded himself to stay clam and breathe easy as the guard circled his truck. When he returned to Maddux's window, the guard tapped on his clipboard with his pen.

"What's even more interesting is that smashed in front end you have. You know it's illegal to cross the border to fix your vehicle."

"It's been like that for a while," Maddux said, thinking quickly. "I've been so busy with work that I haven't had the opportunity to take it in."

The guard didn't flinch. "I'm going to need you to step out of the truck, Mr. Whittaker."

"Is there a problem?"

"Get out, now."

Maddux climbed out of the truck and crossed his arms.

"This damage looks too fresh," the guard said. "Did it just occur?"

Maddux shook his head. "About two weeks ago, maybe less. I can't remember the exact date. A car slammed on its brakes in front of me."

After silently pacing back and forth in front of the truck's grill, the guard finally stopped. "I don't believe you. There's something that doesn't feel right about this."

"I'm not sure what to tell you that will make you think otherwise," Maddux said. "It was just a little collision, but it's fine. The truck still works, and when I get back I plan to get it fixed right away."

The guard looked at one of his men standing nearby. "I want this vehicle searched completely, and if you find anything, I want to know about it. In the meantime, I'm going to find out if Jim Whittaker really works for Opel."

Maddux wanted to protest, but he already felt like he was pushing his luck with the Soviet guards who were running the post. There was no avenue to appeal, not that he would win one anyway. Eyeing the guard closely, Maddux watched him disappear inside the small hut to make a phone call.

Less than a minute later, the guard emerged. "I called someone over at Opel, and they have no record of you attending any meetings there yesterday."

"Who did you speak with? It's not even 7:00 a.m."

"That's none of your concern, Mr. Whittaker. All you need to know is that there isn't anyone there who can verify your story. In fact, the only people there are refuting it."

"But I was there, I swear. I met with Mr. Bernstein, the head of the marketing department in Berlin. You should call him. He will verify that I was there."

"I appreciate your—"

"I found something," one of the other men shouted, stopping the guard from continuing.

The guard hustled over. "What is it?"

"Apparently Mr. Whittaker was also attempting to sneak weapons across the border."

Maddux looked over his shoulder at the two men peering behind the truck's bench seat. There were three rifles and another handgun hidden out of sight.

Maddux groaned and shook his head.

The guard yanked one of the guns out and held it up before shaking it in Maddux's face. "What kind of fool do you think I am?" the guard asked. "Trying to sneak weapons into West Berlin? What a foolish thing to attempt. You're going to prison now."

"What? That's not my—I didn't do anything," Maddux countered.

"Don't lie, Mr. Whittaker. You've already told too many of those."

The guard nodded at one of his subordinates, who hustled over to Maddux and handcuffed him before escorting him to a nearby transport van.

Maddux slumped onto the bench as another guard fastened his shackles to the side of the truck. The head guard sauntered up to Maddux and leaned in close.

"You're going to be staying a little longer than you originally planned, Mr. Whittaker."

Maddux winced as the door rattled shut.

THE EARFUL FROM RABORN only cemented Pritchett's morning as one of his worst since assuming a position of leadership within the agency. But any denunciation he received paled in comparison to the criticism he heaped on himself. He analyzed every conversation, every decision, every hunch, wondering if he would've done just one thing different if there would've been a more favorable outcome.

As it pertained to his most pressing issue—the whereabouts of Dr. Heinrich Schwarz and, subsequently, Ed Maddux—Pritchett mulled over his decision to hire Maddux. Pondering that such a move could've been a mistake, Pritchett recounted just how much he knew about Maddux before engaging him to help root out the potential Russian attack at the World's Fair less than two years ago. Pritchett wondered if he could've achieved the same outcome without soliciting Maddux's assistance. And that led Pritchett to contemplate if the success of the mission clouded his judgment in pressuring his superiors to offer Maddux a more permanent position in Bonn.

Did the KGB get to Maddux? Did they coerce him into doing something? Was there a blind spot that I missed when evaluating him?

Pritchett wasn't letting up on himself in between scrounging around for information and shifting to an alternative plan to capture Schwarz. If Maddux had failed, Schwarz could already be in Moscow, a thought that chilled Pritchett. Pulling the physicist out of Russia would be a far more arduous task than doing it in East Berlin—and someone else would be saddled with cleaning up the mess Pritchett's failed operation had left. And that didn't bode well for his career within the agency.

He made plans to return to Bonn later that evening. With Schwarz's status still in limbo, Pritchett felt the need to get back to his domain. He paced around his office. Stopping to stare out his window, he wondered aloud. "What happened last night, Maddux?"

The phone rang, startling Pritchett. He sauntered over to pick it up, closing his eyes before he did and praying he wasn't about to receive more bad news.

"Have you heard anything else?" asked Rose Fuller.

"I'll give you an update as soon as I hear more," Pritchett said. "But right now, we're all just trying to find out what we can. And so far, nothing."

"I feel so helpless here not being able to do anything."

"Rose, it sounds like you're taking this a little bit more personal than usual."

"Maybe I am, but I can't help but feel that maybe I'm responsible in some way."

"What do you mean?"

She sighed. "I created the tech for the mission.

What if it went wrong? What if something didn't work?"

"You can't beat yourself up over something like that," Pritchett said. "Sometimes things just don't go the way we planned, and there's nothing we can do about it."

"How do you handle these situations then?"

He paused. "Honestly?"

"Yeah."

"I don't do well with this. In fact, I'm giving you advice that I should be taking myself. But I'm too much of a perfectionist to not let it bother me."

"You're speaking my language."

"I wish I wasn't," Pritchett said. "We don't all need to be brooding over what could've potentially gone wrong with this operation—at least not until we hear something back from someone about the whereabouts of Maddux and Dr. Schwarz."

"Well, I'll leave you alone to brood there. Just please call me the minute you hear something."

"I'll do my best to keep you updated."

Pritchett hung up and sauntered back over to the window. He wasn't there more than half a minute before the phone rang again.

"Pritchett," said West Berlin station chief, Jerry Mullins, as he answered the phone, "you need to meet me on the roof. One of our informants just showed up and has some intel that I think might interest you."

Pritchett hung up and hustled upstairs. He dug his hook into the door before he pushed it open, and the bright noonday sun flooded his good eye. He shielded himself from the light and ambled toward the two men standing in the center of the roof.

"What's this all about?" Pritchett asked.

"Meet Dietrich," Mullins said. "He has some information for you."

"Your man is in trouble," Dietrich said. "I heard from one of my Soviet friends at the border patrol that they arrested a man this morning on suspicion of being a spy. Last night, someone stopped a prisoner transport van and freed the man the Soviets were holding."

"And both men got away?" Pritchett asked.

Dietrich nodded. "But two of the guards saw what the agent looked like. And then an American from Bonn showed up at the border this morning in a truck that looked suspicious. The Soviets arrested the agent on the spot for a number of different offenses, chief among them attempting to have his truck fixed elsewhere."

"And the prisoner they were holding?"

"The Soviets still aren't sure where he is."

"Is that all you know?"

"The American agent is being held at the Soviet prison nearby, but they haven't moved him yet and don't plan to until they know more."

Pritchett dug into his pocket and then handed Dietrich a twenty-dollar bill. "If you hear anything else, you'll be sure to let us know."

The man nodded and thanked Pritchett before scurrying away.

"Dammit," Pritchett said.

"I know, I know," Mullins said. "That doesn't sound promising. But on the bright side, at least the Soviets don't have Schwarz yet."

"Anything less than a full recovery of agent and asset is a failure in my book."

Mullins huffed. "You've been doing this long enough to know that not everything goes your way, Pritchett. Just lighten up and try to glean the positives from this situation. I mean, at least you know that your agent didn't stab you in the back."

"That's little consolation at this point when Director Raborn is breathing down my neck."

"Raborn's not the only one," Mullins said.

"Geez, there's someone else?"

"Marvin Watson, the president's private secretary."

"You heard from him?"

Mullins nodded. "This morning, he called me after you spoke with Raborn. Apparently LBJ is up in arms about this deal. He sees the space program as a benign and bipartisan pet project of Kennedy's that the entire country can get behind, so he has an abnormally high interest in Schwarz's whereabouts."

"What did you tell him?"

"Nothing, but don't be surprised if he calls you back and demands more answers. Watson is relentless, and he's going to dog you until he gets an answer that will please the president."

"Why do they have to complicate things like this?"

"It's their job," Mullins said. "They're bureaucrats. They're paid to make everyone else's life miserable."

Pritchett froze for a few seconds. He held up his finger, silencing Mullins.

"What is it?" Mullins asked.

"Didn't Dietrich say that the man crossing the border had a truck?"

Mullins nodded. "So, what do you make of that?"

"Maddux came over in a car, one especially

designed to sneak people back across the border. Maybe that wasn't him."

"Or maybe Maddux had to switch vehicles and get a truck for some reason."

"He wouldn't just ditch something Rose gave him," Pritchett countered. "Those vehicles she outfits are loaded with spy gadgets."

"I bet it's still him," Mullins said. "Something may have gone seriously wrong. But the news could be worse."

"What do you mean?"

"I mean if the Soviets knew who they had, they would've contacted us by now. They're still trying to put the pieces together, which means you still have time to salvage this mission if you work fast."

Pritchett slapped Mullins in the chest. "I think you're right. I need to go make some phone calls."

Pritchett hobbled back toward the stairwell, returning to his temporary office. He shut the door and settled into his chair to make a phone call. Despite all of Mullins's assurances and upbeat predictions about what was going on behind the scenes across enemy lines, Pritchett wasn't convinced all was well.

He dialed a number and waited for the person on the other line to answer.

"Hello?"

"Gil, this is Charles Pritchett."

"To what do I owe the pleasure of this phone call?"

It had been several years since Pritchett spoke with Gil Williams, but these were desperate times.

Pritchett paused for a moment. "I've got some real problems here in Berlin, and I was wondering if you might be able to help me out."

"Does it have to do with the kid?" Williams asked.

"How'd you guess?"

"I figured it's the only way I'd ever hear from you again. Is he putting everything together yet?"

"Not yet, but I need you to see if you can get some information for me about him. Apparently, he's being held in East Berlin, and I need to know about the facility where he would be. I have to get him back home."

"I think I can help you out if you promise me that he doesn't find me."

"I'll do my best."

"That may not be good enough."

Pritchett bit his bottom lip and thought for a moment before responding. "Look, nobody ever thought he would get this far, but I had to give him a file about you. And—"

"You did what?"

"Just settle down," Pritchett said. "He still doesn't know anything, at least anything of substance."

"How can you be so sure?"

"Most of the pertinent information about you was redacted. And he's getting close."

"Nobody can find out about this, Pritchett. If they do, I'm toast."

"I know. I'll do my best to stave him off."

"Fine," Williams said. "I'll help you, but you better not let me down."

Pritchett hung up and hoped he could fulfill all his promises. Every single one he'd made seemed to be weighing on him like a truckload of bricks—and he wasn't sure how much longer he could hold up beneath the weight of them all.

GÜNTER VOIGT STRAINED to hear the conversation taking place in the backseat. He slowed as he approached a traffic light, hoping it would turn yellow so he could justify stopping. The light didn't comply, and he drove through the intersection. At the next crossroads, he got his wish.

Upon returning home to visit with his family for a few days, Voigt received a phone call that he was needed there too. Ivanov had a scheduled meeting in East Berlin and requested Voigt to chauffeur. In exchange for obliging Ivanov's request, Voigt was awarded an extra day off. The arrangement didn't thrill Voigt's wife, but she didn't complain about having her husband around for a little longer.

While Voigt had only been able to hear pieces of the discussion occurring behind him, he had heard enough to know that something notable had just gone down in Berlin. As the car idled while waiting for a green light, he gleaned what was happening: The KGB had arrested an Opel employee from Bonn who they suspected of being a spy. No one knew who the man was as the company denied that the name given by the man was on the payroll.

Voigt recognized an opportunity when he saw one, albeit one that was a long shot given his recent betrayal of the CIA's trust. When the agency first approached him about spying for the U.S., he saw that as an opportunity to make some extra money. Then he considered how he might be able to make more and get extra benefits if he informed his superiors at the KGB of the offer, hoping that they would want him to take it and become a double spy. Voigt's long shot became a reality. And for a while, the perks from the KGB were nice. More frequent visits to East Berlin to see his family, longer stays, and a little extra money. However, over a period of months, he slowly realized the KGB was never going to give him the thing he wanted most in life—freedom.

When Voigt pulled into the Russian embassy, he asked Ivanov for a minute of his time.

"What is it?" Ivanov said, pausing before he exited the vehicle.

Voigt sighed. "It's my wife. I just learned that she is having some health issues now, which require me to be back home to help her. Do you think it would be possible for me to spend a few more days in Berlin to help her with the children while she recovers?"

Ivanov shrugged. "Anything is possible, but you will need to still work for the KGB to maintain your comfortable position here."

"I understand. Perhaps I could drive for the KGB in Berlin."

"We have plenty of drivers for KGB officials, but

I know we are always lacking reliable transport drivers."

"I would be most grateful for anything you could do for me."

"You've been quite helpful," Ivanov said. "I will see what I can do and let you know the outcome later today."

"Thank you, sir."

Ivanov climbed out before slamming the door shut.

Voigt tried not to let anyone see him smile. He waited until he was parked and away from any prying eyes before he unleashed a wide grin.

* * *

THAT EVENING, Voigt thanked his wife for a delicious meal and then retreated to the roof for a smoke. He ignited a cigarette and took a long drag before slowly exhaling a plume of smoke. Throwing his head back, he closed his eyes and mulled over the best way to proceed. Before he could do anything, he had to win back the trust of the Americans, which wouldn't be an easy task. But maybe they would take a chance and let him redeem himself. If there was anything he'd learned while working with both the Russians and the Americans, it was that the former wouldn't tolerate any mistakes, while the latter were quick to give second and even third chances. However, he wasn't sure such grace would be extended to him given the fact that the two CIA agents he duped ended up getting captured by the KGB.

After returning to tuck his children in bed, Voigt told his wife that he needed to go out for a while.

"You're not going out drinking, are you?" she asked.

"No, dear. I've got some business to attend to."

She eyed him closely. "What kind of business?"

"I can't talk about it right now, but I will soon. I promise."

She pointed at the clock. "Don't be late."

"I won't," he said before kissing her on the forehead.

Voigt made his way to a park two blocks away where a competitive pickup game of soccer was taking place beneath dim street lamps. After watching for nearly half an hour, he was relieved when a goal was scored that ended the match. As the men dispersed, Voigt hung in the shadows, awaiting one particular man, who went by the name of Elias. Voigt wasn't sure if that was the man's real name or not.

Voigt remained leaning against a light pole for a few seconds after Elias walked by. Then Voigt casually spun around and started following the man, keeping a safe distance until they turned the corner and stepped into the shadows. After scanning the area one final time, Voigt deemed it safe to make an approach. He gently took hold of Elias's arm.

He stopped and pulled his arm back, twisting away from Voigt.

"Get your hands off me," Elias said. "Who the hell do you think you are?"

"You better be careful with that kind of response out in public," Voigt said. "Someone just might find out who you really are."

Elias's eyes narrowed. "You still haven't answered my question. *Who are you?*"

"A man who needs a favor."

Elias turned and started to walk away. "I don't know what you've heard about me, but that's not the kind of man I am."

"Not *that* kind of favor," Voigt said. "I'm happily married. But I need you to deliver a message for me."

Elias stopped and sighed before turning around slowly to face Voigt. "What makes you think I can deliver a message to anyone?"

"That's your job, isn't it? You're a courier, right?"

Elias shrugged. "I've been known to make a delivery on occasion, but I do other things as well."

"I have an occasion for you to take a note for me to one of your contacts in Bonn."

"And what makes you think I'd do that for you, a complete stranger?"

"You're the only one who can do it for me. And this message is of utmost importance to the people you reach out to."

"The people I contact pay me to deliver *their* messages, not *yours*," Elias said. "Thanks for the offer, but no thanks."

"No, no, no," Voigt said. "I can pay you."

"You think you can afford me?" Elias said, looking Voigt up and down.

"I will pay double whatever you receive for each delivery."

Elias's eyebrows shot up. "Double? That just made your proposition far more interesting. Do you know how much I'm paid?"

"I don't care. Whatever it is, I'll pay twice what you normally receive. So, do we have an agreement?"

Elias stroked his chin and stared off at the skyline

in the distance.

"I'll tell you what. Make it three times my normal rate of 400 Marks and I'll do it."

Voigt closed his eyes and shook his head, knowing his desperation cost him. But he didn't care.

"I'll meet you back here in an hour with the money and the message," Voigt said.

"I'll be ready."

When Voigt returned an hour later, Elias was nowhere to be found. Voigt checked his watch before shoving another cigarette into his mouth. He flicked his lighter and watched the tobacco ignite, the first drag warming his lungs.

After another minute, Voigt noticed a man walking on the other side of the street. He shuffled along, casting a handful of long glances in Voigt's direction. Eventually, he disappeared around the corner.

Voigt went to look at the time again when he felt a sharp object poke him in the back.

"Do you have the money?" the man asked.

Voigt turned around slowly, raising both hands in the air. Standing in front of him was Elias.

"A cordial greeting would've been more appropriate," Voigt said.

"I'm not interested in making friends," Elias said. "I just make the deliveries."

Voigt produced a bag of cash from his coat pocket. "Twelve hundred Marks—it's all there."

"And the message?" Elias asked, holding out his hand.

Voigt handed over a piece of paper. "It's confidential."

"They always are."

Elias turned to walk away, but Voigt grabbed the courier and spun him back around.

"When are you going to make this delivery?"

"Tomorrow."

"And how will I know that you did it?"

"You just have to trust me," Elias said. "If they want to respond, they will."

Elias hustled back around the corner, quickly vanishing into the night.

Voigt pulled out another cigarette and lit it as he stared across the street. He noticed the man who was walking on the opposite side a few minutes earlier had returned. He had both hands jammed into his pockets, his head cocked to the side, and he glared in Voigt's direction.

Voigt waited until the man rounded the corner before heading home.

I can't live here much longer.

MADDUX STARED AT THE SLOP foisted in front of him as he sat handcuffed to a table in the interrogation room. The fact that he was receiving any food at all was a sign that the KGB was unsure who he was working with. But the idea of eating the gray gelatinous substance shimmering in the bowl made his stomach churn.

"Eat up," one of the guards said. "It's good."

Looking up at the man, Maddux attempted to raise his hands only to have them halted by the chains.

"I won't eat it like a dog," Maddux said.

The guard shrugged. "I have my orders. Your cuffs are not to be unlocked."

Maddux cocked his head to one side and raised his eyebrows. "Do I look like a threat to you? I just want to eat something."

Maddux debated internally how he wanted the guard to respond. If the guard stood pat, Maddux wouldn't mind since it'd mean skipping out on having to put the unappetizing mush in his stomach. But if the guard acquiesced, Maddux knew that he might have an advocate should his situation turn dire.

Shuffling over to the table, the guard released Maddux's left hand before re-securing his right.

"Better?" the guard asked.

Maddux nodded, unsure of whether he should thank the man for giving him an opportunity to eat the food. After picking up the spoon, Maddux stirred the porridge and then attempted to eat it. The bland mixture was cold, and he couldn't stand the taste. After two skimpy bites, he set his utensil down on the table.

"You need to eat more," the guard said as he scowled at Maddux.

"Have you ever tried this?"

The guard said nothing as he continued to eye his prisoner.

"If you had, I know you would not be encouraging me to eat this. Feeding people this food is torture."

The guard forced a laugh. "If I have an opportunity, I will show you what real torture is all about."

So much for being my advocate.

Maddux picked up his spoon and shoveled down several more bites before pushing the bowl away.

"Finished?" the guard asked.

Maddux nodded.

"Then it is time to take you to your cell."

Maddux's handcuffs were released from the table, and his left hand was returned to the bindings. With a firm tug on the back of his collar, the guard pulled Maddux to his feet and shoved him toward the door. Stumbling toward the exit, Maddux lost his balance and slid a few feet along the ground before stopping.

"Get up," the guard roared.

Maddux struggled to stand upright, leaning against

the wall to help him regain his footing. The guard tapped on the door, and another man on the outside unlocked it. Forced forward by the barrel of a machine gun, Maddux trudged down the hall.

Once he reached a corridor laden with cell doors, the guard yanked one open. With a swift kick, he sent Maddux sprawling inside, ending with him splayed out on the cobblestone floor.

"Enjoy your stay," the guard sneered before slamming the door shut.

Maddux had heard of the legendary Stasi prison in Berlin, but he never imagined he'd see the inside of it as a prisoner. Lying still on the ground, he closed his eyes and prayed that he was merely having a bad dream. When he looked up, he saw a dim bulb overhead and realized he was entrenched in a living nightmare.

"You American?" asked a man.

Startled by the presence of another person in his cell, Maddux bolted up and scanned the room. He hadn't noticed anyone else when he was thrown inside, but reclining on the top bunk was another man, who looked to be fast approaching sixty years of age, with a full head of gray hair and a weathered face.

"Who are you?" Maddux asked.

"My name's Phil. And you are?"

"Jim," Ed said, still sticking with his alias.

"Well, Jim, welcome to Hell."

"What'd you do to get in here?"

Phil chuckled and shook his head. "You don't *do* anything to get in here as you might already know. You just get *assigned* here. And it depends on who brought you here and how valuable you are when it comes to how long you'll be here."

"You been here a while?"

Phil turned and looked at the wall, which had tick marks etched everywhere. "It's been a while since I tallied them, but I think it equates to about a year and a half. Apparently, there's no urgency to release an engineer whose specialty was building tunnels."

"Is that what landed you in here?"

"Like I said, you don't exactly have to do anything to get tossed into the Stasi. I was in the middle of giving a lecture at the university when I was arrested. Someone accused me of being a spy, and there was no convincing anyone else otherwise."

"I have a similar story."

"Do tell," Phil said, gesturing toward the wall. "From my best guess, we're going to have plenty of time."

Maddux stood and paced around the room. "It's simple really. I came here for work and when I tried to leave, I was arrested at the border for trying to sneak weapons across."

"That's serious," Phil said. "I guess you were doing something."

"But I wasn't really. I borrowed a truck and didn't realize it had weapons in it."

Phil hopped down from his bunk. "Wait a minute. You borrowed a truck from someone that had a weapon in it and they didn't tell you."

"So, maybe I didn't know the person very well."

Phil's eyes widened. "You stole a vehicle."

"No one has accused me of that yet."

"But you did, right?"

Maddux froze, unsure if this random pairing with a cellmate was a ploy. Instead of telling the truth, Maddux decided to concoct a story that wouldn't make him sound so guilty. "I'm sure the guy forgot that he left it in there."

"Or maybe you didn't tell him that you were going to cross the border."

"That may have been part of it too," Maddux said, crafting the story as he went. "I just needed to get something I'd left at the place where I was staying earlier in West Berlin. I didn't think there'd be any problem about skipping back and forth across the border."

"Man, you don't look that naïve, but that kind of defense isn't going to fly with the East Germans."

"I was arrested by the Soviets."

"Oh," Phil said. "That's a different story altogether. You likely won't be here long."

"What's that supposed to mean?"

"I'm not speaking in some cryptic code. All I know is either you're here for a while or you're not. People arrested by the Soviets are usually only transferred here for a short period of time. What happens to them after they leave? Your guess is as good as mine. But based on what I know, I doubt they're being sent to a different prison, if you know what I mean."

"If you're suggesting that they're going to put me in front of a firing squad, I doubt they would do that. I have powerful friends in the government."

"Yeah, well, I did too. Hell, I worked for the government, but that didn't seem to make much of a difference when it came to getting me out."

"What agency did you work for?"

"One with three letters."

Maddux sighed. "You seem to have left that little piece out of your story earlier."

"I wasn't sure I could trust you."

"You still think that?"

"Is Jim your real name?"

"Is Phil yours?"

Phil smiled. "Touche. You're a smart fellow, and I'm quite certain that you're here for reasons other that what you're saying, but I get it. I've been wary of all my cellmates in the past—all thirty-seven of them."

"Whoa, that's quite a number of people they've paraded through here."

"Yeah, it's a little crazy, and I try to think that I'm the lucky one, imagining that all of those men are just being taken out back and shot. But the good Lord has kept me alive for some reason, though I'm still not sure what that's for. Whatever it is, there's got to be a higher purpose in it all."

"So, you're the religious type?"

"Has the world changed that much in the last year and a half that most people aren't?"

Maddux shrugged. "No, I guess not. I just never would've guessed someone could be stuck in a prison and think that God had some plan for something good to come out of it."

"You need to read your Bible more. People were always in prison, wrongly accused in many cases or unjustly placed there. I'm still praying that God will send an angel to unlock the doors and lead me out like he did to Peter."

"A man can dream. Maybe I'll dream about that too tonight."

"In the meantime, I need to catch you up to speed on how things work on the inside here."

"I'm assuming you're using the word *work* very loosely. After all, we're both unjustly imprisoned here."

Phil chuckled. "When I say *work*, I'm talking about how to navigate the system. What I've been able to cobble together isn't ideal, but it works. And as my friend John Hambrick used to say, 'If it ain't broke, don't try to fix it.'"

Maddux froze. "What did you just say?"

"I said if ain't broke—"

"No, who used to tell you that?"

"Just a friend."

"You said his name. John something—"

"John Hambrick," Phil said, eyeing Maddux closely. "Do you know him?"

Maddux nodded. "I've been trying to find him."

"I worked with him for quite a while. Funny thing is, I only said that because you have a striking resemblance to the guy, and it made me think about him."

"I'm sure understanding how this place works is important, but I want to know more about John Hambrick."

A whistle echoed down the hall.

Phil scrambled over to the door leading out of their cell. "Come on," he said. "We have to stand at attention over here or suffer the wrath of the guards."

"Well, I want to know more about—"

"Sshhh," Phil said, glaring at Maddux. "We'll talk about it later. Right now, it's time to be quiet."

"Silence," roared one of the guards as he marched in Maddux's direction.

"That doesn't sound good," Maddux said.

"It's going to be worse if you don't shut up," Phil said. "That's why I wanted to tell you about how this place worked before you got in trouble."

The guard stopped in front of Maddux's cell and spun to face the door. Inserting a key, the guard sprang open the lock before snatching Maddux by his collar and dragging him into the corridor.

"Let's go now," the guard barked.

Maddux glanced back over his shoulder to see Phil with his eyes closed and head down, subtly shaking the latter. With so many questions, Maddux could only hope that he had the opportunity to speak with Phil again.

The guard shoved Maddux to the ground and kicked him, urging him to get back up.

Maddux grit his teeth and followed orders, suddenly concerning himself with a more pressing matter, wondering if he'd even live long enough to have another conversation with Phil.

PRITCHETT THUMBED THROUGH a copy of the *Stars and Stripes* newspaper, his lone connection to life at home in the U.S. All the news was relatively old by the time it found its way into print, but he didn't mind. Reading about sports news was a brief respite from the front lines of espionage that consumed every other waking moment of his day.

"Anything interesting in there?" Fulbright asked as he settled into the chair across from Pritchett's desk.

"Depends on what you find interesting," Pritchett said. "If by that you mean who won this weekend's football games, then yes. If not, I'm not sure I care one iota about the Beatles' new music tour that's making all the young women swoon."

"Be careful not to forget what we're over here doing—protecting every young woman's freedom to faint at the sight of a floppy-haired Brit."

"As long as I have the freedom to change the station when *Help!* comes on the radio."

Fulbright chuckled. "America needs somebody, and not just anybody when it comes to this intelligence war with the Russians."

Pritchett glared at Fulbright. "I'm beginning to wonder if I shouldn't have left you in East Germany."

Dex poked his head into Pritchett's office. "What's going on in here?"

Fulbright grinned. "Pritchett is feeling down but he was telling me how much he appreciates having us around."

Pritchett shut his newspaper and folded it over several times before slapping it on his desk.

"That's enough," he grumbled. "Shut the door."

"I must've missed something," Dex said, following Pritchett's orders before easing into a chair next to Fulbright.

"You didn't miss a damn thing, just the stupid Beatles," Pritchett said. "But we have bigger fish to fry that require our immediate attention."

"Does it have to do with Maddux? Have you heard from him yet?" Dex asked.

"Not exactly, but I think we have some confirmation that Maddux is still alive, but it's from a source I'm not too fond of at the moment."

Fulbright furrowed his brow. "CAShadow-5? Did you hear from him? He's in East Berlin now."

Pritchett sifted through the pile of paper on his desk until he found the folder he was looking for. He opened it up and dug out a note. "I received this note from one of our couriers early this morning," Pritchett said. "It reads: Mr. Fulbright, I apologize for what I did. I had no choice. But I can still be of assistance to you. I heard that the KGB just arrested an Opel employee and is being held at the Stasi. I want to help."

Fulbright leaked a wry grin. "Even CAShadow-5 likes the Beatles."

"This is serious, Fulbright," Pritchett said. "And to be honest, I'm not exactly inclined to believe a single word that he wrote in that note. But I know it's his handwriting and Maddux being arrested would make sense why we haven't heard from him since the exchange."

"But we still don't know about Dr. Schwarz, do we?" Dex asked.

Pritchett shook his head. "That's another question I need an answer to before Director Raborn calls me up and chews me out for another half hour. I can't go on much longer without any report on what's happening over there."

"And you can't send us, can you?" Fulbright asked.

"Under no circumstances can I send either of you back after being captured," Pritchett said. "If I had my druthers, I'd send you both on a lengthy vacation. But I need your insight and experience on this matter right now until we get it resolved."

A knock on the glass interrupted their conversation. Rose Fuller stood outside, clutching a set of files against her chest. Pritchett motioned for her to enter, and she readily joined them.

"Any news yet on Ed?" she asked as she closed the door behind her.

"We were just discussing that," Pritchett said. "Based on a note we received from one of our couriers, a not-so-trustworthy asset currently in East Berlin reported that the KGB just arrested an Opel employee."

"That has to be him," she said, her eyes widening.

"Well, let's not swallow this news whole just yet,"

Pritchett said. "This same asset is the one who got us into this mess in the first place by laying a trap for Fulbright and Dex here."

"CAShadow-5?" she asked.

Pritchett nodded. "That's the one."

"Regardless, this still makes sense that Ed is the Opel employee who would've been arrested. I'm sure if someone else from Opel would've been apprehended in East Berlin, we would've heard about it by now."

"Perhaps, but Maddux was operating under an alias. This could all be part of a ploy to lure us back, maybe even detain more of our agents and exchange them again for Dr. Schwarz."

"But we still don't know where he is, do we?" she asked.

"Not a peep from him," Dex said. "Nor have we heard anything from our listening posts. It's like nothing happened."

"Did you stock the safe house in East Berlin?" Fulbright asked.

"To the gills," Pritchett said. "Both of them could've stayed there for two weeks without having to even come outside."

"And you can't send someone there to check on it?" Dex asked.

"I'm not risking any leaks this time," Pritchett said. "The only people in this agency who know about that safe house are in this room and Maddux. That's it. I have a tight circle."

"I'll go," Rose said.

"You'll go where?"

"To East Berlin to check on the safe house. I mean,

somebody has to do it, and these two are chained to their desks for a while."

Pritchett shook his head. "We need you here, Rose. All your genius ideas and ingenuity is what's helping us win the intelligence race."

"And apparently it was one of my genius ideas that got Maddux in trouble," she said.

"How do you figure?" Pritchett asked.

"If everything I gave him worked properly, there's no way he would've not been back by now. The device I gave him to kill the transport truck's motor, the gas canisters to neutralize the guards, the car to sneak Dr. Schwarz into the country—everything he needed to take possession of Dr. Schwarz and get him back across the border was there."

Fulbright sighed. "Nothing ever goes just like you plan it, Rose. Sometimes things just get sideways out there. It's not always neat and tidy like we draw it up."

"You don't think I know that," she said. "I've been out in the field and know firsthand just how different things can end up. But I'm telling you that something had to go wrong with what I gave Ed. And because of that, I'll gladly go to East Berlin and find out what's going on."

"That's a nice gesture, Rose, but I'm gonna have to decline your offer," Pritchett said. "We can't afford to have you out there."

"You can't afford not to," she fired back. "How much longer before Director Raborn calls you up and lets you have it? You don't think he's going to be demanding any answers from you the next time that phone rings?"

"And if I lose one of our brightest technical minds, the director will be asking me the same thing—and I won't have an answer for either you or Dr. Schwarz. Besides, I'm still not confident that CAShadow-5 isn't up to another trick, playing on our desperation to find out what's happened to Maddux."

"How would he even know that if he didn't know that Maddux had been arrested?" Rose asked.

"She's got a point," Dex said. "CAShadow-5 couldn't even concoct such a plan if he didn't know that Maddux was in the custody of the KGB or East Germans."

"I don't care," Pritchett growled. "That asset just lost all trust I had with him. We'll have to figure out another way to check on the safe house, but it's not going to be Rose or either of you two who will be the ones to do it."

Rose glared at Pritchett. "Sometimes we have to take risks."

"Sending you isn't a risk I'm willing to take," Pritchett said. "Besides, you've probably never heard the stories about what German soldiers did during the war to women—and I'm not about to tell you either, especially since we're mixed company. Just know that it's awful and I'd never forgive myself if you ended up in the Stasi."

Rose pursed her lips and shrugged. "The fact that I'm a woman is all the more reason to send me," she said. "They're never going to suspect me entering their country as a spy."

"The answer's still no," Pritchett said. "And I don't want to hear another word about it."

"Then what are you gonna do?" she asked.

"I'll think of something," Pritchett said.

His phone rang and he answered it quickly.

"Sir, Director Raborn is on the line and wants to speak with you," Pritchett's secretary said.

He put his hand over the phone. "I need you three to leave."

"It's Raborn, isn't it?" Rose asked.

"I'm not changing my mind, Rose," Pritchett said as he shooed them toward the exit with the back of his hand.

Pritchett watched them file out of his office and close the door. He swallowed hard and removed his hand from the speaker, bracing for the unpleasant conversation that would inevitably follow.

ROSE TOOK A DEEP BREATH and calmly handed her passport to the border patrol agent guarding the access gate into East Berlin. She placed her hands back on the steering wheel, gripping it tightly. Keeping her eyes locked on the road ahead of her, she steadied her breathing and waited. To defy Pritchett was going to cost her, but she was confident he wouldn't hold a grudge forever, hoping that he might even thank her by the time everything was settled. But she needed to get into the city first.

"This is unusual," the guard said as he crouched down against the window of her car.

Don't panic. Be friendly.

"What is unusual?" Rose asked.

"We don't have many women crossing the border alone."

"I am here to visit a family friend."

The guard chuckled. "Oh, I understand now. You're here for a *special* visit."

Rose wasn't amused by his insinuation. "It is my late father's best friend who is now just days away from dying."

The smile vanished off the guard's face. "I didn't mean any disrespect. But this is an unusual situation. We're going to need to inspect your vehicle more closely."

The guard signaled for another man to come over. Within seconds, several other guards were combing the outside of her vehicle and checking the trunk. One of the men roamed around the outside of Rose's car, using a mirror attached to a long rod to look underneath.

"Is all this necessary?" she asked.

The guard glanced back down at her passport. "It is if you want to enter the city. Our enemies have been more creative as of late in how they try to get in and disrupt things here. This is all for your protection. I'm sure you understand."

Rose wanted to smile but resisted the urge. "Of course, I understand. But I need to get through here quickly to see my father's friend. If he passes away without me getting to see him one last time—"

She paused and put her finger in the corner of her eye, feigning the wiping of a tear.

The guard stamped Rose's passport and handed it back to her. "Enjoy your visit."

He waved her onward as another guard raised the gate arm.

Rose let out a long, slow breath and eased onto the gas. She didn't feel fully relieved until she couldn't see any of the guards. Pulling over along the side of the road, she dug out her map and plotted her course to the home of Günter Voigt. Once she was satisfied with her route choice, she eased back onto the road and continued on.

Venturing behind enemy lines wasn't a new experience for Rose, but doing so all alone was. She felt most vulnerable, fully aware of the reputation of East German guards and how she would be powerless to prevent any unwelcome advances on her own strength. However, she had a few devices to help her out in case of an emergency. And while she felt vulnerable, she also experienced a newly discovered sense of empowerment. Tinkering with technology from the safety of her lab was easy, but heading deep into enemy territory was terrifying and exhilarating all at once. After she got past the healthy portion of fear, she realized she enjoyed the element of unknown danger that lurked as she tried to accomplish a mission she embarked upon against Pritchett's orders.

Deep down, she also wondered if she would've ever attempted such a treacherous operation had any other agent but Ed Maddux been involved. That thought had been the one that nagged at her the entire length of her drive from Bonn to East Berlin despite her best effort to push such ideas aside. She convinced herself she was here to help Pritchett and Dr. Schwarz—and maybe even Maddux, too. But Rose understood she was quite adept at lying to herself.

After fifteen minutes, Rose slowed down to read the numbers on the apartment buildings. She found the one that corresponded with the address listed in Voigt's file and promptly parked her car in an empty space along the street. While the time was approaching 9:00 p.m., she didn't believe it was too late to pay him a visit at his home. The file on CAShadow-5 was robust, but it never described him as rude. Words like *cordial* and *friendly* and *winsome* were the more common adjectives used by agents in their reports about dealing with him.

She knocked on the door and then clasped her hands in front of her, awaiting the response from the other side.

After a few seconds, nothing.

She knocked again.

This time, she heard voices and the rumbling of footsteps.

When the door eventually swung open, Voigt wore a wide grin, which quickly dissipated in exchange for a furrowed brow, head cocked to one side.

"Can I help you?" Voigt asked.

Rose nodded. "I hope so. I am looking for Günter Voigt."

"You've found him. What exactly can I do for you?"

"Mr. Voigt, we need to talk," Rose said as she glanced over her shoulder. "And we need to do it inside."

He didn't budge. "What's this all about?"

"I'll tell you once we step inside. This isn't a conversation I want to have out here."

Reluctantly, Voigt opened the door wider, allowing Rose to join him in the apartment.

"Dear, who is that at the door?" a woman called from inside.

"Come here and let me introduce you," Voigt said.

Voigt closed the door behind Rose and ushered her toward the main sitting area adjacent to the entryway. She was about to take a seat on the couch when Voigt's wife hustled into the room. She was wiping her hands on her apron when the smile on her face disappeared.

"Who is this?" she demanded.

"Sigrid, this is—"

"Margaret," Rose said. "Margaret Underwood. I know your husband through work in Bonn."

"Do you?" Sigrid asked as she crossed her arms. "And what are you doing here in Berlin?"

"We have some business to discuss," Rose said.

Sigrid arched an eyebrow. "Business? At this time of night?"

"It's all right, dear," Voigt said. "Let's finish putting the children to bed, and we'll all talk about it together." He turned toward Rose. "Make yourself comfortable here, and excuse us for a few minutes. We'll be back to discuss business with you together."

Rose forced a smile and nodded before settling onto the couch. While waiting, she scanned the room to get a better feel for who Günter Voigt really was and what his family was like. Situated on top of a pair of end tables were a couple pictures of his family posing near some beautiful Alpine scenery, everyone smiling. The furniture fabric appeared worn and the wooden legs nicked and fading. Scratches and dents marked the floor, which creaked with almost every step.

If the KGB is paying him, it isn't much—or else he's hiding it somewhere.

Rose heard a door latch shut and the sound of heavy footsteps down the hall. Seconds later, Voigt appeared with Sigrid.

"Would you like some tea?" Voigt asked.

"That'd be delightful," Rose answered.

Sigrid scurried out of the room and began banging around pots and pans before returning.

"It'll be ready in a moment," she said.

"Thank you," Rose said. "Now, getting to our matter of business."

Voigt sat down. "Before we begin, I want you to know you may speak freely here. Sigrid knows what I'm doing."

Rose pursed her lips and looked hard at him. "And what exactly are you doing?"

"All the espionage activities I'm participating in—she's aware of that."

"Does she know *everything* you do?" Rose asked.

"Most of it. Why?"

"Because based on your latest communiqué with the office in Bonn, we need to know if you're still on our side or not. Plenty of people, including Agents Fulbright and Poindexter, were left confused as to whose side you're on in this fight, ours or the KGB's."

He shifted in his seat. "It's not always black and white in our world, as you may know."

"I'm very well aware of that, but springing a trap for our agents is about as dark as it gets, especially if you want us to trust you enough to work with us again."

Sigrid's eyes bulged out. "What did you do, Günter?"

He closed his eyes and shook his head slowly. "It sounds much worse than it was."

Rose frowned. "It's difficult to get much worse than arranging for a pair of agents to get apprehended by the very agency we're trying to subvert."

"Günter!" Sigrid exclaimed.

The pot whistled from the kitchen, demanding her attention. She sprang up from her seat but kept her eyes trained on him as she strode toward the exit.

"Are you trying to get yourself killed?" she asked before retreating to the kitchen.

Rose shrugged. "I guess I'm not the only one who feels strongly about your actions back in Bonn."

"But you don't understand," Voigt said. "I didn't have a choice. If I didn't give them up, they would've suspected that I was actually on the side of the Americans."

Rose pursed her lips. "And that's really the question, isn't it? Whose side are you really on?"

Sigrid returned with a tray with three tea cups and offered one to Rose first. She thanked Sigrid and took one. Sigrid handed her husband one before setting the tray down on the coffee table and rejoining the conversation.

Sigrid patted Voigt on the knee. "Yes, dear, I think we're all interested in whose side you're on."

Voigt sighed and looked down at his drink. "This is not what I wanted, none of it. I just wanted to lead a simple life with my wife and children. But fate had other plans. I was forced to work in Bonn by the KGB. They promised me perks despite separating me from my family. Then I saw an opportunity with the Americans to maybe make enough extra money on the side to one day leave this all behind and go live the way I wanted to. And then everything got complicated."

Rose took a sip of her tea.

"You definitely had a hand in complicating matters. But we can't change the past, and so I'm here to talk about the future, specifically your future."

"What do you want me to do? I will do anything to help."

"That's why I'm here, to assess your loyalty and see if you're going to betray us again or assist us."

"I want to help," Voigt said. "And then I want out. If I help you, will you help me and my family find a new place?"

"I can't promise you anything, but I will speak with my superiors and see what's possible. But regardless, you owe it to us to help after what you did."

Voigt blew out a long breath. "I told you, I couldn't help it. The KGB threatened me if I refused to trap the two CIA agents."

"And now the KGB has another one of our agents, one that you heard about."

Voigt nodded. "And I know where he is—and I can help get him out."

Rose took another drink and emphatically set her cup down on the end table. She stood and clasped her hands behind her back. "Mr. Voigt, I believe I have everything I need to discuss this with the agency and make a determination about how we will move forward with you."

"So, will I hear from you again?" Voigt asked, his voice pleading.

"I won't make any guarantees," Rose said. "That decision is out of my hands. I'm just a messenger here."

"Please, do what you can and know that I am on your side. And, more importantly, I have access to The Stasi. I've been granted an extended stay as long as I transport prisoners for the KGB from East German custody. My first assignment is two days from now. Maybe I can get him a message, let him know you're trying to extract him."

"I will be in touch," Rose said before turning to Sigrid. "And thank you for the tea. Perhaps I will see you again as well."

Sigrid smiled. "It was my pleasure."

Rose headed for the door and waited for Voigt to open it. She bid them a good night and exited the apartment.

Once Rose returned to her car, she drove to a nearby hotel and checked in. Her room was located on the fifth floor, and the elevator wasn't working. Lugging her suitcase up the stairs, she stopped for a moment and froze. She thought she heard another pair of footsteps behind her.

It must've just been an echo.

She made it to the landing outside the door with a number 5 placard above it. After setting down her luggage, she tried to open the door, but it didn't budge. Wedged against it was another person's foot.

Before she could scream, a gloved hand covered her mouth.

"If you're smart, you'll keep quiet," a man said as he pulled Rose's head against his chest.

MADDUX SPIT THE DIRT out of his mouth as he clambered to his feet. He winced in pain, his ribs throbbing from the most recent kick from the foot of the flanking guard. Without giving the men surrounding Maddux the pleasure of seeing him struggle, he forced a half-hearted smile and kept moving.

"You Americans always act so tough, like John Wayne," a guard said, eliciting a jovial response from his colleagues. "Western movies aren't like real life, are they?"

Maddux didn't say a word.

"I said *are they?*" the guard repeated.

Maddux shook his head, and he stumbled forward.

"You're right. They're absolutely not like real life. Because in real life, sometimes the cowboy dies. And we're about to find out if you will soon meet that same fate."

Shuffling along the corridor, Maddux refused to be baited into saying anything that might earn him a few more beatings. He endured several shoves in the back with the butt of a rifle before being led into an interrogation room. One of the guards chained Maddux's handcuffs to the table and then pushed him down into a seat. After the guards exited, Maddux was left alone to get focused for the impending barrage of questions.

A short, stocky man wearing a pair of wireframe glasses and a bowler hat lugged his briefcase up onto the table across from Maddux. Taking a seat, the man opened his case and started sifting through it. He retrieved a large stack of file folders and set it aside with a loud thump. After shutting the case and storing it beneath the table, he fished a cigarette and lighter out of his coat pocket.

"My name is Helmut Hoffman," he said as he ignited his cigarette. "And I am your best chance of making it out of here alive." He slid out a large pad from beneath the folders and scribbled something down on it with a pen. "Would you like to tell me your story?"

"Who are you again?" Maddux asked.

"I'm your advocate with the East Germans. If the Soviets decide that they want to speak with you for some reason, your odds of getting out are—how do you Americans say it?—*slim to none?*"

"Perhaps you can tell me why I'm here because I haven't done anything."

"People don't end up in the Stasi because of what they've done; it's all about what they are capable of doing along with who they really are. And I think you and I both know that your real name isn't Jim Whittaker."

Staying with the legend was Maddux's best opportunity to weather this initial wave of questioning. If he deviated at any point, that would spell the end for him, and he knew it. This conversation would either solidify him as an honest man or as a deceitful spy. Maddux understood that in order to prove he was the latter, he couldn't be the former.

"I'm afraid I don't understand," Maddux stammered. "I *am* Jim Whittaker, and I do work at Opel."

"Or so you say," Hoffman said. "Now I'm not interested in getting into a long, protracted conversation with you. I have questions; you have answers. If you answer me truthfully, we will be able to get through this relatively painlessly and you'll be back on your way before you know it. So, let's begin, shall we?"

Maddux shrugged. "I'll do my best to answer anything you ask."

"That's all I want you to do. Now, let's start again. What is your name?"

"Jim Whittaker."

Hoffman scratched something down with his pen before stopping and casting a long glance over the top of his glasses at Maddux. "Okay, Mr. Whittaker, can you please tell me who is your employer?"

"Opel, the car manufacturer."

"And what do you do for Opel?"

"I work in marketing and advertising."

"So, you are a skilled expert in lying to people," Hoffman said with a smug smile.

"Not exactly, sir. That's illegal, and the company would be subjected to heavy fines if we built our advertising campaigns around claims that were simply proven not to be true."

"I've looked into Opel. Very few of their ads seem to tell the truth. Even your parent company claims to have seen the future. And yet you apparently don't get met with any resistance regarding those silly claims.

Because if GM can really see the future, I doubt they would've assigned you to such an environment."

"That's not what—it doesn't mean—oh, forget it. I'm not sure it's worth explaining to a non-English speaker."

"Try me," Hoffman said.

"Those are both simple phrases we use in the U.S., like the *slim to none* phrase you were trying to come up with a few moments ago. Native English speaking customers understand the difference."

"Yet you employ those same tactics while attempting to sell vehicles beyond the west's oppressive regimes."

"Those phrases don't exactly translate, so we use something else. But all the ads are along those lines. It's not illegal to do what we're doing."

Hoffman stroked his chin. "Perhaps not illegal, but certainly misleading to someone who might see the advertisements as something to be trusted rather than something to trumpet the best features of an automobile in a very figurative way."

"I don't make the rules for advertising," Maddux said. "I simply abide by them."

"Well, the rules we have here are quite different than the ones you have in America. As you might say, we don't take too kindly to outright lies used to sell an expensive piece of equipment."

"All of you people over here have watched way too many Westerns."

"What?"

"Never mind," Maddux said. "The bottom line is I came here as a representative of Opel to meet with investors who are building a list of employees who can run the business in a similarly efficient manner."

"Then how come no one at your headquarters in Detroit have ever heard of you?"

"You called on a weekend. Just because there was no one in the office to answer the phone doesn't mean I'm not an employee. Check back tomorrow, and you will find someone who will confirm my employment there."

Hoffman looked at his sheet of paper and scanned it, checking off various boxes as he moved down the page. "Mr. Whittaker, I'm afraid that I can't help you. Based on what I've heard from you, I believe that you are lying."

"How can you say that? You refuse to wait even a day to call my superiors in America and verify what I'm saying."

"I'm going with a hunch here."

"A hunch? What kind of advocate are you?"

Hoffman raised an eyebrow. "Who said anything about me being your advocate? I said I was your best chance to get out of here, but that chance is a fleeting one. You appear to belong here if I'm the one who must make the decision."

"Well, are you?"

"Am I what?"

Maddux pleaded with his eyes. "Are you the one who makes these decisions?"

"Fortunately for you, I'm not. But that shouldn't be much solace because the people I answer to usually extend less grace than I do."

"And who do you answer to?"

"It's not a who, but a what—the KGB. And if you remain here much longer, I doubt it will be a pleasant stay. They will do everything they can to make your incarceration an unpleasant one. So, if there's anything you would like to revise from your previous statement, I am willing to listen."

Hoffman placed his pen down and then crossed his arms before reclining back in his chair.

Maddux leaned forward in his seat, peering onto Hoffman's paper.

"Actually there is something I'd like to correct," Maddux said.

"Oh," Hoffman said, eyes widening. "Please, do go on."

"I noticed that you spelled by surname with one t, but there are two in my last name. W-h-i-*t-t*-a-k-e-r."

"And that is all you wish to say?"

"There isn't much else left when you've done nothing but tell the truth, especially when you seem more intent on accusing me instead of attempting to make an honest inquiry."

"Very well then, Mr. Whittaker, good luck during your stay here—if you make it that long."

Hoffman gathered his belongings and approached the door. After rapping on it several times, a guard unlocked and opened the door and then ushered Hoffman into the hallway. Maddux couldn't help but think Hoffman was right about him being the sole hope for escaping the East Germany prison, but there wasn't anything that Maddux could've done differently to change Hoffman's mind. Hoffman likely already had a recommendation drawn up before he even entered the room.

Moments later, a pair of guards returned and escorted Maddux back to his cell. One of the men ended the trip by pushing Maddux in the back. He stumbled for a second before regaining his balance.

"Don't worry," one of the guards sneered. "You won't be here long."

The door clanged shut and was locked before the guards began their long walk down the hallway.

Maddux scanned the room for Phil before locating him perched on the top bunk, reading a book.

"Went that well, huh?" Phil asked, looking over the top of his book.

Maddux shrugged. "I guess it's hard to say until something actually happens, but I think it's safe to say that the man interrogating me wasn't persuaded that I was telling the truth. He made some veiled threats about what was coming next to induce me to say more, but I stood firm. I figured it was a ploy and he'd already made up his mind about what he was going to do with me."

"You're right about that last part. Those interviews are always a sham."

"And what about the other part of my statement?" Maddux asked. "You think they're going to transport me out of here?"

"Maybe—if they don't shoot you first."

"You're quite the ray of sunshine today."

Phil chuckled. "Hey, you asked. I speak the truth."

Maddux stood and started to pace. "Well, since you claim to be an honest man, let's just forget about all this for a minute and talk about John Hambrick. You mentioned before I left that you worked with him. What exactly did the two of you do together?"

"We worked for an engineering firm based out of Munich."

"Munich? Now that's a city I haven't heard associated with him since I've been tracing his path across Europe."

"Well, he was there, working with me at an engineering firm called Spectra. We were on a team that helped railroads design more efficient routes through the mountains, particularly when it came to navigating through one of them."

"You made tunnels."

"We made lots of tunnels. It was a dream to be able to create such pathways and then go watch the construction crews implement our plans. Some of the routes we conceived were simply stunning when they were completed."

"How long did you work together?"

"Not long, maybe a couple years. I think we both would've stayed there for the rest of our careers until the incident happened."

"The incident?"

Phil nodded. "We were working on a joint rail line through East and West Germany, and a member of the East German secret police accused our team of working with the CIA to help place radio transponders up along the portion of the route through East Germany. Of course, that created a big political brouhaha. Spectra didn't want any part of it since we were almost finished with the project and acquiesced to the East Germans' demands that they interrogate every single person who had worked on the project. John and I were both brought here. Then the next thing I knew, he was gone."

"Where to?"

Phil sighed. "Well, I can't be sure because all I can go on is what someone told me, but I asked one of the guards about where my former cellmate John had been transferred to, and he told me Moscow."

"Moscow? The Russians got involved?"

Phil forced a laugh. "When aren't they involved in East German affairs? They might as well go ahead and annex the entire country into the Soviet Union to just make it official."

"What would they want John Hambrick for in Moscow?"

"Like I said, I'm just going off what the guard told me, but he said that Hambrick was needed in Moscow. When I asked what that meant, the guard said that the Soviet Union required his services on the nation's nuclear program."

"Nuclear engineering? I thought he was more of a civil engineer."

"I believe he was a civil engineer by trade, but he was also trained in nuclear engineering by the U.S. somewhere. I'm not sure about all the details; I just know he mentioned it to me one time when we were talking about switching fields."

"So he went to Moscow to work on nuclear engineering?"

"No, he went there to run the Soviet Union's entire nuclear program."

Maddux took a deep breath and settled onto his lower bunk. His head was spinning with all of this new information as he tried to process it all. John Hambrick—his father—was running the Soviet Union's nuclear program? It seemed too much to comprehend.

Once the lights were turned out, Maddux eased into his bed and attempted to go to sleep. But his efforts were futile. He couldn't stop thinking about his father and the twisted path he'd taken. Despite receiving a few answers about his father's past, it only led to more questions for Maddux. Was any of this voluntary? How did this factor into his role with the CIA? Was he still in Moscow?

Maddux eventually drifted off to sleep, but he was restless all night. It seemed like barely an hour had passed when one of the guards rattled his stick against the bars to Maddux's cell. He awoke with a jolt, hitting his head against the bottom of the top bunk.

"You were warned," a guard said as he grabbed Maddux by his collar and dragged him into the hallway.

Maddux squinted as his eyes tried to adjust to the light. "What's happening?"

"The KGB wants to speak with you."

ROSE DECIDED AGAINST screaming, choosing to listen to her captor's advice. She detected a tinge of an American accent squirreled away in the man's English, which helped her take an inquisitive posture over an adversarial one. Turning around slowly, she looked directly into the man's eyes.

"Who are you, and what are you doing?" she asked.

He spoke in a hushed, measured tone. "The better question is why are you paying a visit to a home the KGB has under constant surveillance? And how come no one from Bonn told us that your station was sending someone over here?"

"And who are *you?*"

"I'm Van Youngblood, but you can just call me Red."

"Oh, I see," she said, pointing to the wavy crimson tuft on top of his head. "Your nickname is Red. Cute."

"It's time to get serious."

Rose twitched her right wrist, and a knife popped out from beneath her sleeve. She caught the blade and grabbed the handle, holding it in an aggressive position.

"I'm serious," she said. "And I'm only going to ask once more who you really are."

"I'm Van Youngblood, one of the Bonn Station's top operatives. If you don't believe me, just call our station chief, and he'll tell you."

"So, for a moment, let's assume you're telling the truth. How did you know who I was, much less be able to follow me?"

"Because I work for the same agency as you. Your procedure for shaking a tail needs a little work, but it was more or less agency textbook. In the end, it was easy for me to follow you."

"Who lives here?" she asked.

Youngblood smiled. "I watch CAShadow-5's apartment as often as possible. I'm not sure I trust him. Now, let's get back to my original question since it appears that you've deemed me to be a trustworthy soul. Why didn't the Bonn station chief warn us that you were coming?"

"Perhaps because they didn't exactly send me."

"That might also answer my first question, which is far more important," he said. "If you didn't coordinate this operation with us, it stands to reason that you would have no idea just how watched the home of Günter Voigt is."

Rose cocked her head to one side. "How watched is it?"

"The KGB keeps round the clock surveillance on that place, though it can be hit or miss some nights, especially around the holidays. There can be large swaths of time where nobody sees what goes on in there, but for most waking hours when he's in town, somebody has eyes on CAShadow-5's apartment."

"And you think I'm in danger now?" she asked.

"You were in danger the moment you decided to cross that line and enter into East Berlin. But the secret police have a permanent tail on you, assigned to you right after you gained access to the country."

"Just great," Rose said. "And you saw them watching me as I entered CAShadow-5's apartment?"

"Someone is going to question him, but he's more than capable of spinning a convincing story. You're the one who needs to be worried."

She let out a long breath and started talking, almost to herself. "I shouldn't have come. I should've just stayed in my lab and—"

"Your lab?" Youngblood said. "You're Rose Fuller, aren't you?"

She nodded.

"You're a lab tech," he said. "You're not even field trained to know how to handle this type of situation."

"More like the director of the lab, but that's just splitting hairs at this point, isn't it?"

"The point is you shouldn't be here. You clearly don't know what you're doing by putting one of our assets in a compromising situation."

"He said he wants to help us."

Youngblood shrugged. "Maybe he does, maybe he doesn't. But your visit to his apartment is going to make it that much more difficult for him to actually do something. You do realize that now?"

"You've made that fact pretty clear."

Youngblood checked over his shoulder to make sure they were still alone. "I'm still a little bit unclear about why you even came here in the first place. Did this have something to do with Dr. Schwarz?"

Rose hesitated, unsure of just how much she should tell him. The moment he told her his name, she recognized him from a file she'd seen in Pritchett's office. But Pritchett had his reservations about trusting the entire East Berlin station, so she was careful about the information she shared.

"CAShadow-5 said he thinks he knows where one of our agents is being held and is willing to help us get him out."

"Where is he?"

"According to CAShadow-5, The Stasi."

Youngblood winced. "That's not good. But why not let us handle it from here? Why come all the way from Bonn behind your chief's back to do this?"

Rose couldn't divulge the real reason, so she opted for a sliver of the truth. "Because I have feelings for the imprisoned agent, and I wasn't convinced that Pritchett was going to take action soon enough."

"That's quite a risk."

"Yeah and maybe one I regret, but it's too late for that now."

"You need to get the agent out of there, and fast," Youngblood said. "The KGB has control over that facility, and based on my past experience, if there's an agency agent held captive there, the KGB moves rather quickly."

"What do you mean by that?"

"Two, maybe three days, tops before they take action."

Rose's eyes widened. "What kind of action are we talking about here?"

"It's either a transport back to the Soviet Union or—"

Youngblood let his words hang, the implication clear .

"Can you help me get a message back to my station chief?"

Youngblood shrugged. "I don't see why not. I think I can get something to one of our couriers."

"Let the Bonn chief know that we're going to do whatever we can to get our agent out by tomorrow night."

"Tomorrow night? How do you expect to do that?"

"If what CAShadow-5 said is true and if agents aren't kept in The Stasi for long, we don't have much time."

"You're going to need help."

"I'm definitely counting on that. Would you be willing to lend a hand, maybe find another couple of agents who can help?"

"I think I can round up a few guys who'd like to help."

"But strictly off book," she said. "I don't want my station chief to take any flack if this thing goes south."

Youngblood chuckled. "You really are new at this, aren't you? Things always go south. It's just how you handle the fallout that determines if your initial mission is a success or not."

"The president is watching this. Nothing can go wrong."

"It doesn't matter who's perched on your shoulder; nothing will run smoothly. But we'll adapt—that's what we do best."

They set up a time and place to meet the next afternoon to discuss the specifics of Rose's plan before she bid him a good evening.

Once inside her room, Rose collapsed on her bed, wondering if she had been a fool for attempting to cobble together her own mission.

"Pritchett's hands were tied, and he would've never seen me as an option even if I'd begged," she said to herself in an attempt to justify her actions.

It would've been too late. We would've lost a good agent and Dr. Schwarz.

She cared more about the former than she would admit. There was just something about Maddux. Maybe it was his smooth voice and rugged good looks. Or maybe it was the way he was always calm under fire. Or maybe it was just the fact that he wasn't a lifelong agent who had never known much of anything else. Maddux had accumulated plenty of life experience in the civilian workplace, and he brought a little flair to the agency, a twinge of joy in his work. It was certainly a nice change of pace in comparison to the longtime agents who found their tasks menial and had become jaded by peering behind the political curtain. Maddux had energy, fresh ideas, and a hunger to make the world a safer place.

Rose realized Maddux was still relatively green and eventually he would likely drift into the same ruts most of her colleagues had discovered. He'd probably settle into a worn out groove and plod along a career path that took aim at a powerful position behind a desk at Langley, just like all the other agents. But Rose hoped he would be different in the end.

A girl can dream, can't she?

If that dream had any chance to blossom into reality, she had plenty of work to do, starting with how to figure out a way into The Stasi and breaking out Maddux. Despite having a slew of gadgets with her, what she needed more than anything was her sharp wits.

Rose was nearly done with sketching out a plan when her eyes grew wide and she froze.

I nearly forgot about him!

While she wanted to find out about Voigt and gauge his level of commitment to the agency, her other main purpose was to find out if Dr. Schwarz had been placed in Pritchett's secret safe house, something she resolved to do in the morning. Neglecting that portion of her mission was a grave error. She then began to question if she had the wherewithal to pull off an operation that snatched a prisoner from The Stasi. The consequences for missing any details on her ultimate operation wouldn't be nearly as forgiving.

Such a mistake might even be fatal.

MADDUX STUMBLED DOWN the corridor with his hands bound together, dreading another round of interrogation. So far the process had been rather benign, but if the KGB got involved, the situation would get far more intense. He rubbed his eyes with his wrists and braced for a shove in the back that never came.

"You guys have gone soft on me," Maddux said to the guards after the lack of violence.

The guards just laughed gruffly and didn't say a word.

After a couple minutes, they stopped outside a door. One of the guards unlocked it and then pushed it open before gesturing for Maddux to go inside.

"Mr. Creznik, your morning appointment has arrived," the guard said.

Maddux eased inside, awaiting a final push. But he only heard the door slam shut followed by the latch locking tight.

"Please, have a seat," said the man sitting at the table.

Maddux settled into the chair and glanced up at the

clock behind the man. The time was two minutes after six, though Maddux wasn't entirely convinced this was all KGB theater. He wondered if he should've braced for the mind games rather than rough physical treatment by the prison guards.

The man's eyes were locked on Maddux as he redirected his attention from the clock.

"It is indeed this early," the man said. "I prefer to take care of my most urgent business first thing in the morning."

Maddux refused to show any emotion, nodding subtly as he stared at the man.

"Allow me to introduce myself," he said, offering his hand. "My name is Yuri Creznik, and I just might be your best chance of getting out of here alive."

Maddux huffed a laugh through his nose. "Must be a standard line when you first meet with a prisoner."

Creznik chuckled. "We have trained the East Germans well, but they don't really understand what that means. They only use it as a way to win a detainee's trust."

"And what do you use it for?"

"When I say it, it's true." Creznik finger combed the wispy strands of gray across his mostly bald head, returning his focus back to the page. "Now, Mr. Whittaker, let's get down to business. How long have you been working for the CIA? Six months? A year? Two years?"

"I don't work for the CIA. I work for Opel. It's a motor car company and—"

"I know what Opel is. The problem I have is knowing who you really work for."

Maddux leaned forward in his seat. "Like I told the

last guard, if you give the headquarters a call, they'll be able to verify my employment."

"And what about your meeting here? Is there anyone locally who can verify a meeting you had at Opel?"

"I'm sure there is, but I don't know how to get ahold of them. My secretary sets up all the meeting details for me in my appointment book. I just show up when and where I'm scheduled to."

"How come there was no appointment book on you when you were arrested?" From his briefcase, Creznik removed a paper sack out and tossed it onto the table. Folders and other documents spilled out, leaving them strewn across the top. "I've gone over the entire contents of your briefcase, and there wasn't a planner anywhere," he said, wagging a finger at Maddux. "I'm beginning to think that you're lying to me."

Maddux needed to quickly get the discussion back on course as opposed to letting Creznik try to catch him in a lie. If there was one element drummed into Maddux during training, it was that the best lie is often close to the truth. Such a tactic could prove to be lifesaving—and Maddux felt the crushing weight of a lie raveling out of control.

"I'm not sure what happened to it," Maddux said, inventing one more fib before changing the subject. "I had some money stashed away inside in case of emergency. Perhaps one of the guards took it. Please tell me a missing planner isn't the cause of all this misunderstanding."

Creznik grunted and scribbled down a few more notes before proceeding. "This is not a misunderstanding," Creznik said. "I am merely attempting to get to the truth behind your strange behavior, not to mention why you were driving a stolen truck."

"Okay," Maddux said before taking a deep breath. "I will shoot you straight—and before you get concerned that I'm—"

"I know what that means."

"That's right. I forgot that everyone in the communist world is obsessed with American westerns."

"I love The Duke," Creznik said, a wry smile breaking across his face. "No one is tougher than that guy."

"He's just an actor. I doubt he's ever actually had to shoot a gun out of someone's hand before."

Creznik narrowed his eyes. "Have you ever had to do that before?"

"Why would I? I'm in advertising."

"You continue to stick with your story, and that's impressive. But we both know that it isn't true."

"This has all been a big misunderstanding."

"Like the fact that you were attempting to cross the border in a vehicle that did not belong to you?" Creznik asked. "Now, I don't know what you call that in America, but here we call that *stealing*."

"I got into an accident, and I had to get back or else I might lose my job," Maddux said.

"You mean the job that no one can verify that you have?"

"I have a big meeting this afternoon with the head of advertising of my company's European division. I was just trying to get back after a drunk man hit my car. If I'm not there today for the gathering that includes several high-level executives within Opel, I will face serious consequences, perhaps even lose my position."

Creznik huffed. "The consequences you'll face here will be far more serious than anything you would receive for missing a meeting in Bonn. Of this much, I am certain."

"Look, I have some money. There's still time for you to put me on a train and get me home in time for my meeting. I can pay you."

"Bribery is not the way out of this situation, Mr. Whittaker. Only the truth will set you free."

"The truth is I am telling you the truth—but you're not interested in believing it. And that creates a big problem for me. Either you want me to lie and tell you what you want to hear, or you want to catch me in a lie so you can justify detaining me further. Which one is it?"

Creznik frowned. "I have exactly one friend from America who is always trying to force me to choose between two options, as if they are the only ones."

He stopped and chuckled for a moment.

"What is it?" Maddux asked.

"The funny thing is you actually remind me of him. Perhaps you know him."

"America is a big country; I doubt it."

"Does the name John Hambrick mean anything to you?" Creznik asked before leaning back in his chair, his gaze dancing across Maddux's face.

Don't even flinch. This is a ploy.

"Never heard of him," Maddux said flatly. "And he certainly wouldn't be the kind of man I would be friends with. A person like that seems too black-and-white for my tastes. I prefer to dwell in the grey."

"As do I, Mr. Whittaker, as do I." Creznik stood and called for the guards. "Don't get too comfortable here," he said as the men began to untether Maddux from the table. "You won't be here much longer."

"So, you believe me? You're going to release me?"

Creznik started laughing, which devolved into a wheezing cough. He held his hand up while he tried to regain his faculties. "On the contrary. I'm not about to let you go anywhere. I have many more questions for you, but it's evident that we're going to need a more suitable location for that type of interrogation. And I know just the place for it in Moscow."

Maddux swallowed hard as the guards thrust him forward. Glancing back over his shoulder, he peeked inside Creznik's briefcase and noticed a book, one that he'd seen recently. Perhaps it was simply a strange coincidence, but Maddux wasn't about to dismiss anything.

The book was titled *The Last Hurrah,* and it had a black mark down the spine, just like the one he'd seen in that photo of Gil Williams. Maddux's mind whirred as he considered the possibilities. *Was it just a mere coincidence? Was it planted there?* He couldn't be sure of anything.

As he considered all the potential reasons, he froze when he re-entered his cell.

Phil was gone.

ROSE COVERED HER HEAD with a scarf and used a pair of large sunglasses to shield most of her face as she made her way down the stairwell of her hotel. That disguise was enhanced with a small pillow she stuffed in the upper back portion of her shirt and a rickety cane to lean on. Politely nodding at the doorman, she hobbled along the sidewalk and turned at the corner. After walking a block, she boarded a bus and headed toward Pritchett's secret safe house.

Along the way, she mentally reviewed the plan she'd devised. It was patchwork, tenuous at best, if she was honest, but it could be executed. She was just missing one important detail: how to get out of the country.

If CAShadow-5 was to be trusted, he could help spring Maddux from The Stasi during a transfer. And if Youngblood could come up with enough volunteers, she would have the firepower necessary to secure Maddux. However, none of her order-defying stunt with Pritchett would amount to anything if she failed to return Dr. Schwarz back to the U.S.

Twenty minutes later, the bus approached her stop.

Rose, still in character, waddled down the aisle and used the handrail to steady herself as she descended the bus's steps. Once on the ground, she leaned on her cane while scanning the area. After identifying the street corner she was on, she continued toward the safe house.

At one point, she felt as if someone was watching her. She turned to look over her shoulder. Satisfied that no one was spying on her, she entered the building and hustled up the stairs to Pritchett's hideout. With a deep breath, she closed her eyes.

Here goes nothing.

She knocked on the door and waited. The sound of approaching footsteps startled her. She wasn't sure what to expect—an empty apartment was the likely scenario she figured to find. But someone was definitely inside.

"Hello?" she said after knocking again. "Is anyone in there?"

"Who are you?" the man on the other side asked. "What do you want?"

"I'm a friend," Rose said. "I'm here to help."

"Sorry. I can't let you in. You don't know the secret phrase. Please go away."

"I'm not going anywhere," Rose huffed. "And if you don't open up this door, I'll knock it down."

"I wouldn't advise that," he said. "I have a knife."

Rose rolled her eyes before digging through her purse. She got down on her knees and put her face to the ground to see how far away the man was from the entrance. Locating a small container, she pulled the cap off and pulled the pin. With one hand, she used the scarf as a filter across her face. With the other hand, she slid the object beneath the door, sending a cylindrical can inside with enough momentum to reach him.

Three, two, one . . .

She heard a thump. Presumably the man on the other side had collapsed into a heap and was sprawled out on the floor. She knelt back down and pressed her face against the floor to verify the noise was what she thought it was.

Working quickly, she fished out her pick set and managed to get the door open in less than a minute. She locked the door back behind her and then inspected the man lying on the floor. He looked like all the pictures she had seen of Dr. Schwarz. Using her foot, she slid the knife aside and waited for him to regain consciousness.

A couple minutes later, he awoke, startled to see her sitting on a nearby chair and staring at him.

"How did you—"

"Relax, Dr. Schwarz," Rose said. "I'm on your side."

"Maddux told me not to trust anyone," he said, his eyes widening. "But you just—"

"Relax, Doc. I'm on your side. Let's not waste time quibbling over who said what and when."

"But we had a plan all worked out, a passphrase that anyone who approached me was supposed to use. He strongly urged me not to open the door for anyone. He's going to kill me when he finds out."

Rose smiled. "Lucky for you then that you didn't open anything."

"Where's Agent Maddux?"

"You really don't have any idea, do you?"

He shook his head. "I saw him three days ago, and he told me to stay here no matter what. We even devised a little system for how to determine if anyone who comes inside is acting on the authority of Maddux or someone else."

"Think for a second. If Maddux was whisked away to prison before he ever had the opportunity to let others know what your access phrase was, nobody is going to have it. Make sense?"

"How do I know you're not lying?"

"You're still here, aren't you?" she fired back.

"Nobody's going to kill me," Dr. Schwarz said. "I'm not wanted dead or alive—only alive. I'm more concerned about my family."

She nodded resolutely. "We'll clear up that mystery for you when we get back on friendly soil. In the meantime, I need you to be ready to leave this evening when I return and give you further instructions. We're going to get you home."

Schwarz forced a smile. "If you say so, but we need a new pass phrase. How about we use 'the good die young?'"

"If you insist, but nobody is dying today if I can help it. Instead, I want us all going home. How does that sound?"

"Wonderful," he said. "What's the plan?"

"For you? Just stay put. I'll send someone to get you when it's time, and be ready to do whatever we ask."

"I'm a rocket scientist," Schwarz said. "I tend to need more information than you simply urging me to go along with whatever plan you've concocted but refuse to share."

"Honestly, I'm still working out some of the details, but leave that to me and the other agents who are developing this plan."

"I hope you know what you're doing," Schwarz said. "I only went along with this because I felt obligated to help out Agent Fulbright for all he did for me and how he treated my family with respect."

Rose sighed and look skyward. "Just be ready, will you?"

He nodded.

"Good," she said. "I'll see you later this evening."

* * *

AN HOUR LATER, Rose stopped two blocks away from Voigt's apartment and searched for a willing subject. She found one in a young boy eager to make twenty Francs for simply slipping a note under Voigt's door. The message was simple: Meet me on the roof in fifteen minutes.

Rose was seated against one of the many chimney stacks that sprouted out of the top of the building. Eyeing the door to the stairwell, she waited for Voigt to make his appearance.

Come on, come on.

She scanned the area once more, wondering if there were multiple ways to access the roof and she'd missed one of them. But after a few minutes, Voigt emerged.

He crouched low as he hustled over to her position.

"What kind of dress is this?" he asked.

"I'm trying to protect both of us."

He studied her up and down. "I'm not sure that's

going to work. You're going to stick out here. Old ladies dressed like you don't exactly get out very often. If someone saw you earlier and now sees you here, they're going to know."

"I might as well be invisible," she said. "No one will give me a second glance. Trust me. I've been in this get up all day long, and not a single person has even raised an eyebrow while looking at me, if they've even taken the time to notice me at all."

"And that's not usual for you?"

"Not really. I guess it depends on how much time I spent fixing myself up. If I look like I'm ready for a fun night of dancing out with friends, I get longer glances. But when I just leave straight from the office? Nobody even sees me. I'm pretty sure I could walk up to someone, stick a knife in them in a busy marketplace, and nobody would see it happen, even if people were looking right at me. It's a gift."

"Yet they've placed you in a basement lab. You must be one hell of a scientist."

"All you need to know is that I run a lab *and* I'm a woman. That ought to answer your question."

"Well, when it comes to being out in the field, don't get too confident—because the KGB invented paranoia. Before you leave this country, you'll be questioning your-self and the presence of every person you met during your time here, wondering if any one was an actual spy contracted to kill you. You'll probably ponder shooting me at least a half dozen times if this crazy plan of yours works."

"This plan is only going to work if you make it work."

"No pressure or anything," Voigt said with a

chuckle. "What do you want me to do?"

"I need you to break the Opel employee out of prison."

He stared at her, mouth agape. "Break him out of prison, as in The Stasi?"

She nodded.

"Have you lost your mind? That place is crawling with guards. I wouldn't stand a keg's chance in a biergarten of making it out unscathed, much less alive."

"The KGB is going to move him very soon. All you have to do is be the one transporting him."

Voigt blew out a long breath and tilted his head back, resting it against the brick chimney behind him. "Just because I have access to The Stasi doesn't mean I can go pick and choose my assignment tonight."

"Work out a trade with another driver. Get creative. You can figure something out between now and this evening, I'm sure."

"And what if they move him?"

"Then I'll be the one who will have to get creative."

Rose reviewed the rest of the plan with Voigt, instructing him on how to signal if he had Maddux. Then came the question Rose was dreading.

"And how are we going to get over the border? Have you thought about that yet?"

"I'm still trying to come up with a plan."

Voight smiled. "Well, I already have one for you. It's tailor made for an escape consisting of a large group. We'll be able to disappear into West Germany before anyone can do anything about it."

"And how are we going to do that?" she asked.

"I was hoping you would ask me that."

XXI

FOLLOWING AN EARLY DINNER, Voigt and his wife, Sigrid, directed their six-year-old son Stefan and eight-year-old daughter Petra to the living room for a family discussion. Voigt sat in a chair, facing the couch where everyone else sat. He leaned forward as he prepared to begin.

"Stefan, Petra—I need you both to trust us tonight. We are going to be going on a special trip later, and we need you to pack your bags with clothes and no more than three of your favorite toys that you want to keep."

"Is this going to be a long trip, Papa?" Petra asked, batting her saucer-like blue eyes at him.

"I'm not sure how long it will be, but we won't be coming back here," he said.

"Not coming back?" Stefan asked. "Where are we going?"

"Some place safe, dear," Sigrid said. "We're going to a place where your father doesn't have to leave us for weeks at a time. We can all be together all the time."

"That sounds wonderful," Petra said before leaping off the couch and running into her father's arms.

Voigt's face spread into a wide grin as he embraced

Petra, her hug confirming that he was making the right decision.

"We won't be able to leave until later tonight," Voigt said, "but I want everyone to be packed and ready to go as soon as I return home from work. Is that understood?"

He watched as both children nodded.

"Excellent. Now, run along and get ready. Your mother has already pulled your suitcases out of the closet and placed them in your room. She'll help you in just a moment."

He enjoyed hearing the joyful pitter-patter of feet racing down the hallway. Both kids shouted something, an obvious signal that they were excited about the forthcoming adventure.

"Still think we're not doing the right thing?" Voigt asked Sigrid.

She stood and meandered over to him. He pulled her in close and gave her a long, passionate kiss on the lips.

Sigrid drew back and cocked her head to one side. "What was that for?"

"You really are the best wife a man could ever ask for," he said, taking her hands in his. "Not only have you given me two beautiful children, but I know that you are willing to take this risk so that we can all have a better life one day soon."

She pulled her hands back, breaking Voigt's grip. "But robbing a train? Do we have to really do that in order to escape? Can't there be some other way?"

"If there is, I haven't thought of it. And the problem is we simply don't have enough time. We need to escape before the secret police decide that they need to tighten security, especially on everyone who even gets close to the border. You know they will."

She sighed. "I trust that you're right, but that doesn't make it any easier to accept. We will be leaving our home, abandoning everything we've ever known."

Someone rapped on the door outside, interrupting their conversation. They both looked at each other with a blank stare.

"Go help Stefan and Petra pack," he said. "I'll handle this."

Voigt waited until Sigrid had disappeared into the back of the apartment before peering into the peephole and checking to see if he knew who was knocking on his door. He'd never seen the man before, but Voigt knew the type.

He opened the door. "May I help you?"

The man smiled politely. "My name is Anatoly Kozlov with the KGB, and I'd like to ask you a few questions."

Voigt gestured for the visitor to come inside.

"Thank you," Kozlov said. "This won't take long."

"Is there a problem?" Voigt asked as he closed the door once Kozlov was inside.

"We received a report of some suspicious activity here over the past couple of days that I need to ask you about."

Voigt arched an eyebrow. "Suspicious activity? What do you mean by that?"

"There was a woman who stopped by here yesterday who is from Bonn. We found that situation to be not so coincidental, given that you work in that city."

Voigt knew he had only one direction to go with the inquiry that might explain the visit to the KGB agent. Voigt looked over his shoulder toward the hallway and then back at Kozlov before speaking barely louder than a whisper.

"My wife is still here," Voigt said. "But that was my crazy girlfriend, if you know what I mean."

"We had no record of you engaging in any such activity while on your duties in Bonn."

Voigt smiled. "There are ways to hide some things from the KGB, especially things you don't care about."

Kozlov narrowed his eyes and took a step closer to Voigt. "Nothing goes unnoticed, though sometimes certain situations are ignored. And we had no record of you ever meeting with a woman like that."

"Perhaps someone left it out of a report."

"If she has traveled from Bonn to Berlin to pay you a visit, I doubt it would've been an inadvertent omission on any of the reports we have about you. Now, who was she?"

Voigt closed his eyes and subtly shook his head. "I already told you," he said, his voice dropping back down to a whisper. "She's my mistress—or was. I can't have her visiting my home with my wife here."

"That woman was here for a long time," Kozlov said as he pulled out a pad and scribbled down some notes. "I'm sure your wife would've seen her."

"My wife didn't see anything. I told her that it was a salesman and that I'd step into the hall to handle it."

Kozlov rubbed his chin with one hand and eyed Voigt closely.

Before any further conversation ensued, Stefan raced

into the room, holding a stuffed animal in each hand.

"Papa, can I take both Oliver and Detlef on our trip?" Stefan asked, holding up the pair. "I already packed two, but I can't leave both of them."

Voigt forced a smile. "Run along back to your room. I'll come help you in a minute."

"A trip—how interesting," Kozlov said. "Where are you planning on visiting, especially since you are scheduled to work for the next few days?"

Voigt's mind whirred as he thought up a plausible explanation. "My wife is taking our children to visit her parents in Dresden."

"That's curious timing since you are rarely home to be with your family."

Voigt shrugged. "The trip was planned before I received this elongated stay here, and their visit is only for a few days."

Voigt watched Kozlov closely to see what he might do next. He crossed his arms and stared past Voigt.

"Let's see if your wife can corroborate your story," Kozlov said. "Call for her to come in here."

Voigt swallowed hard. "Sigrid, would you please come in here and talk to this kind gentleman."

"Just a moment," she said from across the hall.

Awkward silence filled the room as they waited her arrival. After a brief delay, Sigrid strode inside and approached them.

"What do you need?" she asked.

"This is Anatoly Kozlov. He has some questions for you."

She shook his hand and forced a smile. "Questions regarding what exactly?"

Kozlov cleared his throat. "I understand you're going on a trip," he began. "Where are you going?"

She cut her eyes over at her husband, who shot a quick glance at the picture on the wall behind where Kozlov was standing. And she knew immediately how to answer. "To see my parents in Dresden."

"And how long will you be gone for?"

"A few days," she said before furrowing her brow. "I'm really sorry, but what's the relevance of all these questions?"

Kozlov ignored her as he stared down at his notepad.

"And you're all going?" he asked once he looked up again.

"My husband can't go because he's working, but we won't be gone long. We'll see him again very soon."

"I see."

Voigt relaxed as he noticed the tension dissipate from Kozlov's face. The KGB agent seemed as if he was resigned to leave the inquiry alone and move on. He turned toward the door and paused once he grabbed the handle.

"I appreciate the time and—"

"Papa, I packed your bag for you," Stefan said, dragging a bag into the living room. "I even put your favorite stuffed animal inside, too, so you can have one in case you get scared."

Voigt knelt down next to Stefan and tousled his hair. "Son, you know I'm not going on the trip, as much as I'd like to."

"But you said—"

"That's enough," Voigt said. "Go back to your room and play until we're done in here."

"But, Papa—"

"Go now. I won't tell you again."

Voigt turned around to see Kozlov tucking his notepad into his coat pocket, his eyes locked on the little boy leaving the room.

"Perhaps I should also speak with your son?" Kozlov said.

"That won't be necessary," Voigt said. "He's just a little boy. He gets confused sometimes and—"

Voigt stopped talking when he saw Kozlov reach for his weapon. Instead of standing by passively, Voigt engaged Kozlov in an effort to prevent him from gaining any type of advantage. A weapon trained on Voigt would most certainly result in a lost opportunity to escape as well as a possible trip to prison.

Using his right forearm, Voigt battered Kozlov in the head. Caught off guard by the move, Kozlov fumbled his gun onto the floor. Voigt then kneed Kozlov in the face, sending him staggering backward. He hit the wall, allowing him to maintain his balance and respond by storming toward Voigt.

Kozlov put his head down and used his shoulder to drive Voigt into the floor.

"You've made a terrible mistake," Kozlov said before delivering a pair of punches to Voigt's face.

Voigt reached up with his hands and gripped Kozlov's neck, choking him for a few seconds. Struggling to break free, Kozlov spun to one side and slid his knee up to pin down one of Voigt's arms. Kozlov slapped the other hand away from his neck and used Voigt's own tactic.

Kozlov squeezed Voigt's neck hard and watched as he gasped for air.

"You are a traitor," Kozlov said, his eyes narrowing as he stared at Voigt.

Voigt felt his strength slipping away with each passing second. All he wanted was a deep breath and an opportunity to turn the tables on the KGB agent. But desire was being crowded out by ability. Voigt couldn't shake Kozlov.

Head pressed against the ground, Voigt glanced over at Sigrid. He didn't want her to see him die like this, especially after she had been less than enthusiastic about him working for the KGB. He expected to see tears pouring down her face as she endured the pain of witnessing her husband's death. But that's not what he saw at all.

Sigrid knelt on the floor a mere eight feet away, both hands wrapped around Kozlov's gun, the barrel trained on his head. Her eyes were focused on him as she squeezed the trigger.

The bullet ripped through Kozlov's chest, spattering blood against the near wall. He slumped to the ground, remaining ever defiant as he tried to crawl toward them.

Voigt took the gun from his wife and shot Kozlov once more in the head. He collapsed, dead almost instantly.

Looking at Sigrid, Voigt saw her lips quivering as she put her hands to her face.

"What have I done?" she said. "What have I done?"

Voigt put both hands on her shoulders and stooped down to get eye level with her. "You have just saved my life and saved this family," he said. "I killed this agent, not you. I'll never regret it either—and neither should you."

He then embraced his wife, pulling her close as she buried her head in his chest and sobbed.

"It's going to be all right," he said, stroking her hair.

His moment of comforting Sigrid was interrupted by the thundering footsteps coming down the hall. Stefan and Petra froze as they emerged from the hallway and stared at the dead agent in the middle of the room.

"Are you okay, Mama?" Petra asked.

Sigrid sniffled and withdrew from her husband's arms. She nodded and tried to mask her crying.

"It's okay, Mama," Stefan said. "We love you."

"Children, go to your room," Voigt said. "I will come talk with you in a moment."

Voigt glanced at his watch and sighed.

"What is it?" Sigrid asked.

"I need to get going. I'm supposed to begin my shift in about an hour. We need to clean this up immediately. And I'll let you finish packing."

"I don't know if I can do it, Günter," she said.

"I know you can. What happened here is tragic, but I need you to be strong—for me and for Stefan and Petra. We still have a chance to make a new life for our family, but it won't happen if you can't forget about this for a few hours so we can do what needs to be done."

Sigrid blew her nose. "I can do it. I can do it for our family."

Voigt didn't waste any time getting to work. With plans to leave that night, he didn't worry about disposing of the body. Voigt dragged it into the bathroom and hoisted the corpse into the tub. When he returned to the living room, the faint sound of sirens on the street below gave him reason to pause—Sigrid, too.

"They're coming for us," she said. "I just know it."

"Don't worry," Voigt said. "If they do, I'll handle it."

They returned to their work, scrubbing the floor and cleaning Kozlov's blood off the wall but froze when there was a stern knock at the door.

Voigt wiped his hands with a nearby rag and stood. He shot a sideways glance toward Sigrid.

"I told you," she mouthed to him.

Voigt strode toward the door and paused to examine the person rapping on it. Located on the other side was a pair of police officers with their hands on their hips and their heads hung.

"The police," Voigt mouthed to Sigrid.

Her eyes bulged out before she scrambled back to work. The officers knocked again, identifying themselves as members of local law enforcement.

"Stall them," Sigrid whispered.

Voigt nodded and then waited until one of the officers raised up his knuckles to pound on the door again before swinging it open.

"Good evening, gentlemen," Voigt said. "Is there something I can help you tonight?"

"As a matter of fact, there is," one of the officers said. "Mr.—"

"Voigt. Günter Voigt."

"Well, Mr. Voigt, can you please explain to us why people heard gunshots coming from your apartment?"

Voigt grasped the top of the door firmly and stood in the small opening, blocking either officer from getting a clear look inside.

"There must be some mistake," Voigt said. "I didn't hear anything like that, and we certainly weren't shooting any weapons in here."

"We'll see about that," the officer said as he pushed his way past Voigt and entered the apartment.

XXII

ROSE ENTERED THE WAREHOUSE that served as a staging center for CIA operations in East Berlin. With the extraction of Maddux requiring precise timing, she couldn't afford to be late. She glanced at her watch before striding over to a small table where two men sat. The second hand swept past the twelve as the clock read 7:00 p.m.

"We've been expecting you," one of the men said with a smile as Rose approached.

"Are you the one we have to thank for this?" the other man said, holding up a small device.

She took the object and studied it for a few seconds before nodding.

"That's one of my inventions, enabling you to hide your listening device beneath someone's telephone." Rose handed it back to the man.

"It looks just like one of those rubber feet on the bottom of the telephone," he said. "Nobody would ever consider checking there."

The other man offered his hand to Rose. "This is Darby, and I'm Bull."

She shook both men's hands and took a seat.

"Where is Youngblood? He's supposed to be here by now."

Bull shrugged. "It's not like him to be late."

"We need all hands on deck if we're going to pull this off tonight," she said. "I happen to know that the president has requested updates as soon as they're available regarding Dr. Schwarz's status."

"What does this guy do?" Darby asked.

"Space program," she said. "He's apparently irreplaceable when it comes to rocket science."

"So, we're saving the next Einstein?"

Rose nodded and glanced down at her watch again. "Do you know how to contact Youngblood?"

"You can call his apartment," Bull said. "And if that doesn't work—"

"Then what?" she asked.

"Just call him first before we do anything else. He told us that you were being followed, so I wouldn't want to blow his cover."

"You don't have to worry about that any more," Rose said with a wink. "I took care of that this morning. Now, write down his number for me, and I'll try to reach him."

Two minutes later, Rose was standing in a phone booth, dialing Youngblood's number. She counted eight rings before she decided to hang up and return to the warehouse.

"He's not answering," she said after she strode through the door.

"Maybe he's on his way and is running late," Darby said.

"You know Youngblood is always on time unless he has a good reason," Bull shot back.

"Well, maybe he has a good reason," Darby said.

"Good reason or not, none of it is going to matter if he doesn't show up here soon. The timing of this mission is critical."

"What about CAShadow-5?" Bull asked. "Isn't he supposed to be here by now?"

"I told him to be here at 7:30. I wanted us to have a little bit of time to discuss different contingencies without him in case his intentions are to sabotage our escape across the border. But looks like we won't be able to do that now since Youngblood is still missing."

Bull scribbled down directions to an address and then handed the slip of paper to Rose. "He only lives five minutes from here in an apartment around the corner," Bull said. "I would go myself, but agency protocol dictates otherwise."

"I understand," she said, studying the directions. "I'll be back shortly. Hopefully with Youngblood in tow."

She hustled outside and walked swiftly down the street. Given the situation, running seemed more appropriate, but she couldn't risk attracting any attention, especially with all the East German citizens eager to inform authorities of any suspicious activity.

Once she identified the building, she climbed the steps to the fourth floor and then knocked on Youngblood's apartment. When she did, the door budged, creaking as it opened slightly.

Rose eased inside, careful not to touch anything.

"Youngblood? Are you here?" she called out.

She was barely past the hallway before she gasped and then covered her mouth. Her instinct was to scream, but she held it in.

Slumped against the wall was Youngblood's body surrounded by a pool of blood. His throat had been slit, his once white dress shirt now crimson. With furniture strewn across the apartment, she deduced there had been a struggle, perhaps a surprise attack. But the *how* didn't matter at this point. The agency had lost a good man, likely because he dared to warn Rose. And now her mission was in danger of never even getting off the ground.

Rose exited through the back stairwell and took a circuitous route around the building as she returned to the warehouse. Someone had been watching Youngblood, and she realized the need to be extra careful was now critical.

"Did you find him?" Bull asked as Rose hustled across the vast space to the table tucked in the back.

She nodded slowly, waiting to speak until she could break the news gently.

"That look isn't good," Darby said as he stared at her.

"He's dead, isn't he?" Bull asked.

Rose eased into an empty chair and looked down. "I found him, but he was already gone. The bastards slit his throat."

Bull pounded his fist on the table and let out a string of expletives. Darby stood and paced around the table, shaking his head.

"We're done," he said. "We need to shut this down."

She looked at her watch. It was 7:40 p.m.

"Still no sign of CAShadow-5?" she asked.

"Nothing," Bull said through clenched teeth. "I can't believe this."

"I think you're probably right, Darby," Rose said. "This op isn't going anywhere."

THE EMPTY CELL FELT haunting in some ways. Maddux couldn't shake the fear that Phil was planted there, designed to extract information while they whiled their time away in The Stasi. Maddux hadn't been in the espionage world very long, but he'd been there long enough to know that trust was something only to be given away to those who earn it. Tossing it out to people simply because they were knowledgeable could prove to be a grave error. And now Maddux had plenty of time to brood over his mistake.

The day dragged on, interrupted only briefly by the delivery lunch, a stale piece of bread and lukewarm split pea soup.

Later that afternoon, a guard approached the cell.

"Jim Whittaker," he said.

"Yes?" Maddux replied.

"If you have any belongings in here, you need to pack them up and prepare to be moved later this evening."

"Belongings," Maddux said, bewildered. "We're allowed to have personal items with us?"

"You aren't," the guard said.

"But why even tell me that?"

"You will be relocated to a holding area later this evening."

Maddux frowned. "Will I still be in this prison?"

"Just be ready," the guard said with a growl.

"Wait. Before you leave, can you tell me where Phil is?"

A subtle smile leaked across the guard's face before he turned and walked away.

"Come on, sir," Maddux said. "You can't tell me anything?"

The guard kept walking away but held up his right index finger and wagged it high in the air.

"I need someone to talk to in order to stay sane."

The guard continued his long jaunt down the corridor amid a chorus of whistles and boos.

Maddux sat on the edge of his bed and wondered if maybe Phil had left something behind. Searching under the mattresses and attempting to loosen any cinderblocks that weren't still firmly affixed into the wall, Maddux's quest quickly ended in vain.

As someone who dealt in information, this position was a difficult one for him. He didn't know anything other than what he was told—and he didn't believe much of that either. But the fact that he was being moved meant something was going on. Maddux hoped it was more than just the reconfiguring of cell space, but not of the more permanent variety.

Several hours later, a guard returned and ordered Maddux to grab his belongings and exit the cell. Maddux obeyed, entering the hallway with empty hands.

"You don't have anything to take with you?" the guard asked.

Maddux shook his head.

The guard slapped handcuffs on Maddux.

"It's just as well. The less you have, the more likely they will leave you alone."

Maddux furrowed his brow. "Who is this *they* that you're talking about?"

"Your new fellow cellmates."

"I'll have more than one?"

"You'll have more than you can handle. I promise you that."

Maddux shuffled his feet, wanting to extend his time outside this new impending cell. The longer it took him to arrive, the better. At least, it seemed that way from how the next place was described.

Once they exited one corridor, they trudged down another until they came upon a large room cordoned off by three cinderblock walls and one with iron bars. At first glance, Maddux estimated at least fifty men were scattered around the cell, which seemed self-contained. There were a couple tables in the middle that had seating for about a dozen or so people. In one corner was a pair of toilets. Along the far wall were about twenty bunks stacked three high. A couple benches along the near wall gave the prisoners a place to sit when they weren't re-laxing on their beds. But there was no denying that the quarters were cramped.

One of the guards unlocked Maddux's handcuffs and then opened the door for him.

"Gentlemen, here's some fresh meat for you," the guard said before using his foot to shove Maddux.

Maddux stumbled forward before losing his balance and landing sprawled across the tiled floor. He turned his head to one side, staring at the dingy floor. Upon attempting to push himself up, he was met with a strong resistance in his upper back. Dropping down, he pushed up again only to be denied.

Maddux turned slowly to look up at a bald, burly man wearing a white tank top and a full beard. Straggly hair covered his chest.

"Did I say you could get up?" the man asked.

Maddux frowned, puzzled by being met with such hostility. He attempted to roll over, but the man didn't move his foot, keeping Maddux pinned to the ground. Turning to look around the room, he noticed the guards had left.

"Ready for some more fun?" he asked as he panned around the room.

Maddux's question was answered with hoots and joyous shouts.

"Don't make me do this alone," he bellowed.

Within seconds, Maddux was suffering a barrage of kicks and punches. He wriggled free enough to curl up into a fetal position, covering his head with his arms. After a few seconds, the violence stopped almost as quickly as it had started. Maddux's sides ached, and blood oozed from a cut on his arm. But he had withstood the opening salvo from the man in charge of what amounted to a prison gang.

The man knelt down next to Maddux.

"Having fun yet?" the man asked.

Maddux glared at his tormentor. "Is this how you greet all your new inmates?"

The man recoiled, delivering a blow to Maddux's face.

Several minutes later, when Maddux awoke, he groggily staggered to his feet and looked around the room. Half the men were gone. The other half were carrying about their business as if nothing had ever happened, as if Maddux didn't even exist.

"What is this place?" Maddux asked one of the other men.

"We're all about to be transferred—if we're lucky."

"And the man who led the others in beating me to a pulp?"

The sound of several simultaneous gunshots echoed from down the hall.

"He just got shot," the man said. "One of the guards owed the big man a favor for hospitalizing a fellow guard."

"So, I was the favor?"

"More or less. The big guy wanted to beat up an American before he died. I guess you were the lucky subject."

Maddux stopped and thought for a moment. "What did you mean when you said that we're about to be transferred *if we're lucky?*"

"There are only two ways out of The Stasi," the man said. "They either move you or kill you. So, if you're lucky, they move you. Unless they're taking you to one of the gulags in Russia. In that case, you'd be better off standing in front of that firing squad just outside."

Maddux tried not to let his mind wander and get too anxious about which option he would receive. Neither was one he wanted to settle for.

He felt someone tap him on the shoulder. Curious, Maddux turned around only to be met by a fist that slammed hard into his face, knocking him out.

AS THE PAIR OF SECRET POLICE officers forced their way into Voigt's apartment, he wondered if he could shoot them both before they could draw their weapons. Voigt concluded that he wasn't a killer, even if he did pump the final bullet into the KGB agent's body. It wasn't personal—it was survival. And in Voigt's mind, the distinction was important.

But these two fellow East Germans were simply following orders, likely acting on the tip from a concerned neighbor. Did they really deserve to die? Voigt couldn't answer that question yet, but it didn't really matter since he wasn't in a position to go on the offensive. With his gun safely hidden in his closet, such thoughts were little more than fanciful wishes. He had to deal with their inquiry quickly in order to keep the mission—and his dreams of permanently escaping over the border with his family—alive.

The first officer introduced himself as Maier, while the accompanying man went by the name of Jung.

Maier scanned the apartment before addressing Voigt again. "It is our understanding that a KGB agent visited this apartment earlier today. Is that correct?"

Voigt nodded. "I work with the KGB in Bonn, but I came home for a few weeks to be with my family. I'm still working for them while I'm visiting here and have to report shortly."

"Okay," Maier said. "What happened while he was here?"

"We talked and then he left. It wasn't terribly interesting."

"And what did you discuss?"

"My assignments here and what I will be doing for the next two weeks. Like I said, it wasn't all that interesting."

Maier shrugged. "Sounds harmless. But we'll still need to take a look around, if you don't mind."

Voigt understood that Maier was being polite, but he wasn't actually asking for permission. He was being polite in announcing what he was about to do, but Voigt had no viable option to refuse.

Maier and Jung fanned out and began meandering around the apartment.

"Is anyone else in your family here?" Maier asked.

"My wife is giving my son a bath, and my daughter is playing in her room."

"I see," Maier said as he approached one of the closed doors. He didn't knock, instead easing his way inside.

Petra sat on the floor, playing with one of her dolls.

Maier stepped over her and then opened the closet. Clicking on his flashlight, he inspected the upper shelves and then sifted through the clothes. He studied each item before raking it aside and repeating the process.

"What exactly do you hope to find?" Voigt asked.

"There was a report of a gunshot fired in this home," Maier said. "I'm searching for any such evidence."

"In my daughter's closet?"

"You would be surprised how people use their children to shield illegal actions. I'm simply being thorough."

Voigt followed Maier back into the hallway and froze upon seeing Jung entering the master bedroom.

"You might want to knock," Voigt said.

Jung shot Voigt a sideways glance before entering.

Voigt watched as Jung went through drawers, peeked under the mattress, and lay prone to check beneath the bed. He even tore through the clothes in the closet, tossing several outfits to the ground.

"Try to be more considerate," Voigt said. "I'm going to have to clean all of this up."

Jung ignored the request and continued. After coming up empty, he walked over to the bathroom door.

"Please wait until my wife is finished giving my son a bath," Voigt said as he stood behind the officer. "Stefan is really modest and doesn't like—"

Jung barged inside, swinging the door open. He glanced around the room before looking down at Stefan, who was wrapped in a towel while Sigrid tousled his hair. With a gasp, Stefan grabbed his towel and pulled it more tightly around him. Sigrid also feigned a look of shock.

"Who are you?" she asked. "And what are you doing in my bathroom?"

"Pardon me, but we're just responding to a report that there were gunshots fired here," Jung said.

"Well, someone was mistaken," Sigrid said.

Stefan started to speak. "Mama—"

A sharp pinch on his buttocks sent a clear and direct message.

"Gave you a bath," Sigrid said, picking up where he left off. "Yes, I'm sure the nice young man can see that."

Jung panned around the room once more, while Voigt stood behind praying that the officer didn't venture over to the tub and see Kozlov's dead body.

"Sorry for the interruption," Jung said before closing the door.

Relieved, Voigt exhaled slowly.

"Is there anything else you would like to see before letting the reporting neighbor know that he wasted your time?" Voigt asked.

Both officers moved methodically down the hallway, removing pictures from the wall to inspect behind them.

"I really do need to get to work soon," Voigt said.

"Just doing our job, Mr. Voigt," Maier said.

Once they finally reached the front of the apartment, Maier turned to Voigt. "Sorry for the intrusion and the misunderstanding."

Voigt forced a smile. "Thank you for being brief. Now, I must get going."

"We must also," Maier said, offering his hand to Voigt.

Voigt was shaking Maier's hand when Jung spoke.

"Just a moment," he said as he spotted something near the wall. "I want to look at one last thing."

Jung knelt next to a rug and studied the layout of

the room. Scowling he stood back up and walked around the area.

"This doesn't seem right," Jung said as he turned to Voigt. "Has this rug always been in this position?"

Voigt shrugged. "I think so. Why?"

Jung knelt down and lifted the edge of the rug back with his hand.

"This is unusual," he said.

"It's just a rug," Voigt said, his heart starting to thump hard.

"But who places a rug here? It's off center."

Voigt forced another smile. "I was cleaning up for my wife."

Jung ignored him and yanked the rug back. Before he could point out the obvious blood stain that would lead to another line of questioning, Voigt lunged for Jung's weapon, pulling it clean from the holster. Voigt wheeled around toward Maier, training the gun on him.

"Put your gun on the ground," Voigt said.

Following the instructions, Maier eased his weapon onto the floor and then raised his hands into a surrendered posture.

"You're making a big mistake," Maier said.

"Perhaps," Voigt said. "But it'll only be the second biggest one I've made tonight, maybe even the third."

Calmly, Sigrid emerged from the hallway, holding some rope.

"Where's the dead body?" Jung asked.

Voigt narrowed his eyes. "It's about to be six feet in front of me if you say another word."

He switched places with his wife, letting her keep the two secret police officers in her sights while Voigt secured them with the rope on opposite sides of the room. Once he was finished, he explained the next steps.

"I'm not a murderer, and neither is my wife, but she won't hesitate to shoot you if you attempt to scream for help or try to get loose. And I will warn you that she's a pretty good shot. Your chances of surviving are very low. If you comply with these instructions, you'll live. If not, my conscience can't be any more seared than it already is. Nothing will come between me and my family—nothing. Is that understood?"

Both men nodded.

"Good," Voigt said.

He kissed Sigrid on the cheek and then headed toward the door. He stopped and looked at her once more.

"I'll return later this evening. Be ready to go when I arrive."

She nodded, holding her gaze on her two prisoners.

Voigt exited his apartment and looked at his watch. He didn't have much time before he was scheduled to report for his shift. He needed to run.

XXV

ROSE LOOKED AT THE CLOCK on the far wall, cringing as each second ticked past. Her entire operation was about to turn into an unmitigated disaster without Voigt. While he was scheduled to contact her nearly an hour ago, she could only hope he was still making his way to The Stasi.

The shortwave radio on the far side of the room crackled, signaling that someone was trying to reach her.

Since being appointed the head of the Office of Technical Services for Europe, she had been placed in charge of overseeing the CIA's network behind enemy lines. The idea was that in the event of another world war or other conflict, strategically placed radio operators would be able to forward information and other messages over the airwaves to the allies. She requested Hans, one of her handful of East Berlin radio operators, the one who made regular deliveries to The Stasi as a produce delivery driver, to assist the mission.

Hans had hidden an audio transmitter in the guard booth at The Stasi and was supposed to report about any activity he heard there that related to the transport of prisoners.

"What is it, AirMan-7?" Rose asked as she picked up the radio.

"I thought you might want to listen in for yourself," Hans said. "Someone is reporting for duty."

"You're a little early," said one man.

"Better than being later," another man said.

"I don't even have you scheduled for another half hour, Mr. Kloss."

"I'm eager to get started on my shift."

"Trouble with the wife again?" the guard asked.

"More than you'll ever know."

"Well, we might be able to get you home early tonight. There's an American that they want to move as soon as possible, and the other driver hasn't shown up yet. Go talk to the scheduling guard, and see if he'll move you up on the schedule. Anything to score a few points with the boss, right?"

An engine hummed before roaring and then quickly faded. Rose chewed on her bottom lip, unsure of what move to make next.

"That doesn't sound good," she said. "That wasn't Voigt, but it sounds like that driver may be moving our man."

"I wasn't sure what you wanted me to let you know about since I'm unfamiliar with all the people involved in this particular situation," AirMan-7 said.

"Just keep feeding me this information as you receive it," Rose said.

"Wait a minute," he said. "There's some more activity at the gate."

AirMan-7 patched the feed through so Rose could listen in.

"Mr. Voigt, you are right on time," the guard said.

"Punctuality is important," Voigt said.

"Your assignment will be given to you inside."

"I was told that you would have that for me, something about an American spy."

"Check with the scheduling guard. What I have changes so often throughout the night. We've got so many of those damn Americans; they're like flies around here."

"And I've got one of the Americans tonight?"

"Maybe. Depends on what Berger wants you to do. Kloss was trying to get out of here early and might be the one to transport him."

"Kloss," Voigt said, contemplatively. "Is he the one with the red beard?"

"That's the one. He's also missing part of his ear, bitten off during a street brawl. Just don't ever ask what Kloss did to the other guy. I still have nightmares when I think about it."

Rose clenched her fist and glared at the speaker. Grabbing the mic, she opened the channel to respond to AirMan-7. "Is there any way you can get a message to CAShadow-5?"

"Negative. I only have access when I'm assigned to drop something off."

"And you couldn't convince them that you forgot part of an order or something?"

AirMan-7 sighed. "There's not enough time for me to get over there. Plus, I don't even know what he looks like, much less how I would find him. My access only extends from the parking lot to the back entry to the kitchen. I'm not a trained operative."

"I know," Rose said. "Just keep listening. If you hear anything else worth reporting, please let me know."

Rose ended the transmission and wandered back toward Bull and Darby.

"What was that all about?" Bull asked.

"CAShadow-5 may not be able to collect the package. It feels like it's falling apart before it even gets off the ground."

"There's no shame in canceling it if you sense this is going to end badly. Better to live to fight another day."

Rose shook her head. "We just need to improvise a little bit."

"So, we're short one operative—who is now dead—and we don't know if our driver is going to be able to pick up our asset?" Bull asked.

"That sums up our issues for now, but I can fill in for Youngblood."

"And the other problem with the driver?"

"He knows this operation is his best chance to escape. You think he's going to botch this?"

Bull rubbed his bald head before answering. "It's not a matter of if he's going to botch it but if some details might be out of his control."

"Desperate people will go to desperate measures—and that's what I'm counting on."

"Unless he's setting us all up," Darby said, joining in the debate.

"That's always been a possibility," Rose said. "But I got the sense that CAShadow-5's intentions are genuine. He's trapped and wants a better life. And he's smart enough to know he won't get it here."

"I'll go along with this," Bull said. "Anything to

save one of our own, but I think we need to tread cautiously and not hesitate to back out if this goes south."

"Are you still in, Darby?" Rose asked.

Darby nodded. "I'm with Bull no matter what."

"Then let's get going," Rose said. "We need to get ready for CAShadow-5. If he comes through for us, this whole operation will start moving very fast."

XXVI

PRITCHETT HAD JUST REMOVED his eye patch and pulled the bed covers taut when his phone rang. He grumbled as he let it ring three times while debating if he should answer. He preferred going to bed around 9:00 p.m., claiming that he needed the extra sleep to rise early and begin working in his office before 7:30 a.m. each day Everyone at the Bonn station knew the only reason to call him this late would be a death or a major emergency. After a short contemplation, he snatched the receiver off the hook.

"This better be important," Pritchett growled.

"Does a call from the president's personal secretary count?" the man on the other end replied.

Pritchett recognized the voice right away as one belonging to Marvin Watson. "Marv, how the hell are you?"

"I'd be a lot better if Lyndon wasn't breathing down my neck about that Nazi scientist."

"You do realize it's late on this side of the Atlantic?"

Watson chuckled. "I'd have to get in to work too early to reach you in your office. Besides, you know I always enjoy getting under your skin."

"You have a special talent when it comes to that department."

"Look, I'm sure you want to get back to bed, so I'll try to keep this as brief as possible. The president is looking for some information on Dr. Schwarz, that's all. I want to be able to tell him something, anything to get him off my back about this."

"I'm afraid you're going to be disappointed, Marv. I've got nothing. My operative that was supposed to extract Dr. Schwarz and take him across the border is missing. Even worse, I received a message from a courier in East Berlin with a note from one of our assets, who may have been the one to double cross our agents that were captured and then offered in exchange for the scientist. The asset said that our operative was arrested—and I have no idea regarding the whereabouts of Dr. Schwarz. He could be dead for all I know."

"If you don't know where Dr. Schwarz is, let's not suggest that he's dead. Those things are going to make Lyndon blow his top. He really wanted to let those agents twist in the wind because of the importance he's placed upon the space program, but the idea that you could extract everyone quickly following the exchange gave him the confidence to allow the swap to happen in the first place."

"We're all upset around here too, maybe even more so," Pritchett said. "The agent we sent to get Dr. Schwarz has proven to be a valuable one for us. The only shred of hope I'm holding on to is if the agent sprang Dr. Schwarz from the prison transport as he was directed to do, the KGB would've already contacted us with an offer to exchange our agent for Dr. Schwarz again. But then again, the KGB could have both of them."

"Do you think it's possible Dr. Schwarz isn't in KGB custody?" Watson asked.

"I can't say anything definitively at this point since I'm flying dark here, but I'm hoping they don't."

"And you don't have anyone there on the ground to deal with this situation?"

Pritchett sighed. "Actually, I do. We have an agent there right now who is attempting to assess the situation. She went to evaluate one of the other assets we have there who's claiming to be able to help us. He's also the same asset who thrust us into this predicament."

"Tread lightly, my friend."

"Trust me—we are. And that only makes evaluating these types of situations all the more difficult. We need to get Dr. Schwarz back across the border as soon as possible, but I don't want to get more agents caught up in this debacle and have us giving away some of the best Russian spies we've captured. I already feel like we've lost on this one."

"So, you're saying that I can tell Lyndon that we have an active operation trying to get Dr. Schwarz home."

"I don't care what you tell him, but that is pretty close to the truth."

"Why only close?" Watson asked.

"The agent who's there isn't exactly a trained operative—and she went there against my orders."

Watson laughed. "So you have an agent who's just like a younger version of yourself?"

"I wouldn't exactly character her like that, but I guess that could fit."

"Well, keep me posted. There have been some new developments in the past few days, which are responsible for sending Lyndon into this fit."

"What happened?"

"Apparently, the Russians are making considerable strides in their space program. They're about to test a rocket that could potentially get them all the way to the moon."

"But if they have Schwarz working with all these great minds, it might as well be a foregone conclusion."

Watson groaned. "And Lyndon knows it. He doesn't want to lose the space race to those commies."

"So he's counting on us to be his savior?"

"More or less."

Pritchett let out a string of expletives. "This isn't exactly going to help me get any good sleep tonight."

Watson sighed. "Welcome to my world. It's like this every single day. When Lyndon starts brooding, it's all over. He's not going to be satisfied until he hears an answer that he likes."

"And Dr. Schwarz is the topic of the day?"

"Space is the subject—and he wants the U.S. to be there first. He's worried about the fallout if we aren't the first people there."

"Like he's going to lose the next election?"

"Mmhmm. Exactly," Watson said. "I've told him that I don't think the American people care about when it happens as long as it actually does happen."

"I understand—and I agree with him. The American public won't like seeing the sickle and hammer whipping in the lunar wind before the stars and stripes. It's about pride."

"And control of the atmospheric space above the earth. If the Russians get there first . . ."

Watson didn't finish his sentence, but Pritchett understood the inference clearly.

"Look," Watson said, continuing, "just find out about Dr. Schwarz. Give me something, anything. I need to give Lyndon an update tomorrow. Do you think you can let me know something within the next twenty-four hours?"

"I might be the one calling you in the middle of the night in that case," Pritchett said.

"I don't care," Watson said. "My wife is used to being woken up by the phone ringing in the wee hours of the morning."

"In that case, I'll make sure to call you the second I learn anything else."

"Thanks," Watson said. "And good night, Charles. I hope you have some sweet dreams."

"That's doubtful now that you've meddled like this, but I'll do the best I can."

Pritchett hung up, but he knew the call was going to keep him awake all night. He decided the best course of action was to get up, put on a pot of coffee, and start strategizing about another option in case the operation Rose cobbled together failed. He didn't want to think about the kind of repercussions he would suffer for such an action, so he didn't.

But he knew whatever the consequences, they wouldn't be good.

MADDUX OPENED HIS EYES, his vision still blurry from the bone-jarring hit he absorbed to his face. With his entire head throbbing with pain, he remained in a prone position. The room was relatively silent, which hadn't been the case before. Pushing himself up off the ground, he stood and attempted to regain his bearings. He was in the same place he was before getting punched, but the room was nearly empty.

He headed directly for one of the benches against the far wall and sat down. After a quick scan of the room, he realized he didn't recognize any of the previous men who had attacked him or anyone else. Another prisoner seated a few feet away on the end of the bench sat hunched over, eyes closed. One man was doing sit-ups, while another was stretching as if preparing to race.

Maddux rubbed his eyes and then looked up to see a familiar face.

"Phil," Maddux said, "what are you doing in here? I thought you were—"

Phil chuckled. "I thought I was a goner too. It takes a special talent to survive in The Stasi for this long. But

I guess I have all the resiliency of a cockroach."

"Whatever it takes."

Phil sat down on the bench to Maddux's right.

"Yeah, well, I'm not sure what's going to happen to me next now that I'm here."

Maddux furrowed his brow. "They didn't tell you what they were doing with you?"

"The guards around here typically don't, especially if they're about to shoot you. It's too personal, I guess."

"But you don't know what they're doing to you for sure, do you?"

Phil shook his head. "They could be moving me somewhere, but after all this time? That doesn't seem to make as much sense to me."

"You have to stay positive, at least that's what I'm telling myself. I'd fight my way out of here if I could."

Phil leaned around to get a closer look at Maddux's face. "Looks like you already tried."

"That was from a little while earlier. I wish you would've been around to stop it. Apparently, one prisoner's last wish was to beat up an American. Lucky me."

"I bet you can handle yourself. Why didn't you fight back?"

"It wasn't exactly a fair fight. This guy had several other friends help him. Fortunately, the incident didn't last long. I'm not sure why, but they stopped almost as quickly as they started."

The man at the end of the bench injected himself into the conversation. "He stopped because I made him stop."

Maddux and Phil turned toward the man.

"What did you say?" Maddux asked again, unsure if he'd heard the man accurately.

"I said he stopped because I made him stop."

"Then I guess I should thank you," Maddux said. "I didn't realize that man would listen to anyone who wasn't holding a weapon."

"Adolf doesn't typically listen to anyone, but I warned him that his family is in danger if he doesn't listen to me."

"I appreciate the gesture, sir," Maddux said. "But why would you do that for someone like me?"

"I detest needless violence. Please understand that I am a violent person, but only when there is a purpose to it. Seeing such brutal displays makes me ill."

"What's your name?" Maddux asked.

"Beck," the man said. "Franz Beck."

"Well, your kindness is noted, and I'm very grateful."

"In a place like this, you need more friends, not more enemies."

All the men turned when they heard the jangling of keys just outside the cell door. Three guards watched as another guard attempted to unlock it. The gate groaned as it swung open. Two guards strode toward Beck and Phil, taking one each by the arm.

"Where are we going this time?" Phil asked.

"Shut up and walk," the guard said, urging Phil forward.

Maddux watched his two companions trudge down the hallway without another word. Phil shot a quick glance back, his eyes pleading.

Maddux had more questions for Phil.

"Keep your head up," Maddux yelled, resulting in a subtle nod from Phil.

A few seconds later, they had all disappeared around the corner.

Maddux sat on the bench by himself, wondering when the guards would march in and take him as well as which corridor they would take him down.

He didn't have to wait long to receive his answer.

Fifteen minutes later, two more guards entered the holding area and snatched Maddux to his feet.

"Put your hands behind your back," one of the guards said.

Maddux complied, grimacing as the handcuffs were cranked down hard on his wrists. The guard used his rifle barrel to direct Maddux out of the room and into the hallway.

"Where am I going?"

The guard grunted, sounding somewhat amused by the question.

"They never tell me where prisoners are being taken. I just drop you off at processing station. But there are only two choices—and I can guarantee you won't like either one of them."

Maddux stared down the darkened hallway and said a short prayer underneath his breath. If he was alive, he figured he'd always have a fighting chance. And that's all Maddux wanted—a chance.

VOIGT WASTED NO TIME parking his vehicle and rushing to check in with the supervising officer over prison transport. Michael Berger sat at a large desk just outside a staging area, studying documents on a clipboard. Voigt cleared his throat to garner Berger's attention. He looked over the top of his glasses at Voigt.

"May I help you?" Berger asked.

"Günter Voigt—I'm here to report for my assignment this evening."

Berger dropped his paperwork and pushed his glasses up on the bridge of his nose.

"That's right. You're Mr. Voigt, the KGB driver from Bonn. I heard all about you."

"Hopefully they were all about what a safe and reliable driver I am."

Berger shrugged. "More or less, though I don't worry about that too much these days. A guard rides in the front with all the transports, while we have twice as many guards as prisoners in the back, especially for important captives."

"Would my assignment tonight include any important prisoners?"

Berger chuckled. "You act like it's a badge of honor. Trust me, you don't want it."

"I thought I was supposed to transport an American spy tonight?"

"Anyone telling you *that* was using the word *spy* in general terms. The man I originally assigned for you to drive was some advertising agent from Bonn, but Kloss needed to get home to his wife, who's pregnant and in the middle of a meltdown. You understand, I'm sure."

Voigt nodded. "So how does that effect me tonight?"

"I've got a couple of other prisoners who need to be transported to an undisclosed location to be shot and have their bodies disposed of in a most humane manner—by letting nature take care of them."

"You feed the bodies to animals?"

"More like we simply dump the dead and let the wild creatures decide what they want to do with carcasses. It's a very natural process."

"Please don't throw my body into the woods."

Berger smiled. "Then don't get shot, and we'll all get along just fine. Now, where was I?" He sifted through several documents until he found a route for Voigt. "This should answer all your questions," Berger said, handing Voigt a piece of paper. "Be ready to pick up your prisoners in about half an hour."

Voigt nodded and pocketed his orders drawn up by Berger. But there was a new problem and not much time to solve it.

Walking swiftly toward the exit, Voigt scoured the

building in search of Kloss. His red hair and beard along with a shredded ear was sure to make him stand out in a crowd. Voigt reached one area of the building away from all the prisoners and found the guard break room. However, there were more than guards enjoying the area.

Men were situated around tables, partaking in a card game or downing vodka. After working with so many Russians, Voigt had long since shrugged off their practice of drinking hard liquor while on the job. Such behavior was not only accepted but condoned within the KGB, a custom that had taken hold with the agency's East German brethren. However, drivers were the only ones who were discouraged from participating.

Kloss apparently didn't receive that message—or perhaps he didn't care. The chances of anyone saying something to Kloss were minute. He threw back a shot glass followed by a laugh that bellowed throughout the room.

Voigt approached Kloss, settling down into the seat next to him.

"Any chance you will trade assignments with me?" Voigt asked. "I need to get home to my wife, and Berger said he didn't care if you didn't."

Kloss furrowed his brow as he studied Voigt. "Who are you again?"

"Günter Voigt. I'm just here on a short-term basis from Bonn. Trying to patch things up with my wife and have a two-week stay here while working a few transportation assignments."

"You drive for the KGB in Bonn?"

Voigt nodded.

"Must be nice, especially the part where you're away from your wife."

"Actually, that's what I find the most difficult."

Kloss threw his head back and laughed heartily. "You don't have to pretend that you are the world's greatest husband here. Nobody cares. Just be honest. Say it's wonderful."

"I also have two children."

Kloss shook his head. "An even better reason to be working far away. You don't even have to deal with them. If you think you have a bad deal, you aren't a very intelligent man. Besides, I used the excuse about having to get home to my pregnant wife already. But I'm not going home. I'll be hitting the town hard, if you know what I mean."

Voigt exhaled, exasperated over the fact that he couldn't persuade Kloss through a cordial request. Creativity was now required.

While remaining quiet for a few moments, Voigt listened as Kloss bragged about his new car and how many women he'd been able to convince to join him in the backseat. Voigt got up and slipped outside. He heard Kloss make a disparaging remark while walking down the hall. The room erupted in laughter.

We'll see who's laughing in a few minutes.

Based on Kloss's description, the brand new banana yellow NSU Spider was easy to spot in the employee parking lot. Voigt wrote the tag number down and sauntered back inside a few minutes later. Kloss was still in the same chair, surrounded by a host of other employees anxious to hear the next story of his conquests.

Voigt cleared his throat and began his announcement. "May I have your attention, please," he began. "I was just in the parking lot, and I noticed a car with the license plate number HA KC 145 with its lights still on. I'm not a car expert, but I think it was a spider."

"What color was it?" one man asked.

"Yellow," Voigt replied.

Kloss put his knuckles down on the table and pushed himself up. "Excuse me, gentlemen. It seems that I may have inadvertently left my lights on. I'll be right back to tell you all about Helga and her headlights."

The men erupted in laughter, urging Kloss to make his return a speedy one.

Meanwhile, Voigt walked quickly toward the parking lot. He exited and then scanned the area. He didn't notice anyone milling around and determined that his plan was cleared to commence.

Voigt had already engaged in far more violence than he cared to for one day, but at this point, what was one more?

He hustled over to his car and grabbed the tire iron out of the trunk. Crouching low, he worked his way toward Kloss's car.

A few seconds later, Kloss entered the parking lot. He found his car and then threw his hands up in the air.

"What is this? Some kind of joke?" he said aloud.

Voigt rushed toward Kloss from behind and hammered him in the knees with the iron. Kloss's knees buckled as he fell forward. He was in the act of rolling over to his back when Voigt connected with Kloss's head, resulting in a skull-cracking sound.

Kloss fell limp, his eyes shut.

Voigt wasn't sure if he had killed Kloss or simply knocked him out. Either way, Voigt had succeeded in his overall objective. He worked quickly, dragging Kloss's enormous body across the pavement to the back of his car. Voigt rooted around in Kloss's pocket to find the keys. Once Voigt located them, he unlocked the trunk and heaved Kloss's body inside. Feeling for his pulse, Voigt sighed—though slightly relieved—when he realized Kloss was still alive. Voigt retrieved the syringe Rose had given him and drove it into Kloss's neck. According to Rose, an injection would leave an average-sized man incapacitated for as long as two hours. Voigt figured Kloss would awake in about an hour and a half.

Before closing the trunk, Voigt fished the assignment orders out of Kloss's pocket. And there was only one piece of information that interested Voigt:

Prisoner name: Jim Whittaker

Voigt was startled by the sound of a guard's voice.

"Who's over there?" the man asked as he pointed his flashlight in Voigt's face.

"It's just me," Voigt said, raising his hands. "I came back to get something from my car."

"That doesn't look like your car," the guard said.

"I was just walking across the parking lot, and I was trying to read this order."

"Well, you better hustle back inside. Employees aren't supposed to be loitering out here."

"I understand," Voigt said as he nodded toward the guard before hustling back inside.

He walked immediately over to the holding area.

"I'm here to pick up a prisoner," Voigt announced.

"Papers," the guard said, holding out his hand in a nonchalant way.

The guard took the documents and studied them for a moment.

"You're not Kloss," the guard said.

"He told me I could have his assignment. We swapped."

"Then where is he?"

"I saw him in the lounge, throwing back shots of vodka."

The guard huffed and shook his head. "Why does everyone always make it so difficult?"

"I'm here to make things easy for you," Voigt said. "I'll take both our assignments and spare you the lecture from your commanding officer."

The guard eyed Voigt cautiously. "I can't do that."

"Why not?"

"The ratio would be off. We're required to have at least one guard for every prisoner—and in some cases, two guards for every prisoner."

Voigt shrugged. "Well, I'd have three prisoners and three guards."

"But you need four."

"Is it really going to matter? Have you seen these guys? Do you think they could challenge any of our guards?"

The guard exhaled, the strong odor of alcohol coming off his breath.

"I'll tell you what," Voigt began. "I'm usually stationed in Bonn and I can get the good stuff, the kind I bet you prefer over this Russian garbage."

The guard furrowed his brow and cocked his head without saying a word.

"Don't play dumb with me," Voigt said. "Your breath reeks of the stuff."

The guard put his hand over his mouth, turning red since he'd been busted by Voigt.

"Two bottles," the guard said sternly. "You better honor your word or I will make your life miserable when you return."

"I wouldn't lie about such a thing," Voigt said.

The guard stamped the papers and then strode through a door, disappearing for a few seconds. When he emerged, he handed Voigt some papers.

"Two bottles," the guard said, holding up a pair of fingers for emphasis.

"I won't let you down," Voigt said sincerely, as if he actually meant it.

"Pull the designated vehicle to the loading dock in the back. The keys should be in the ignition."

Voigt nodded and headed to the lot where the transport fleet was stored. He handed his documents to the guard, who glanced at them before handing them back and waving Voigt through.

Once Voigt found the truck, he drove it around to the loading area and backed into the designated spot. After throwing the vehicle into park, he hopped down and walked over to speak with the man in charge of dispatching the various prisoners.

"What do we have here?" the man said as Voigt approached. "Looks like we've got some fresh meat."

"Just lending a hand while I'm home from assignment," Voigt said as he gave the papers to the man.

"How many are there in here? Three prisoners? I can't get six guards in there, too. And that's our policy."

"It's already been approved."

"I don't care if God signed this with a lightning

bolt, I'm not bending our rule for a rental driver."

"Look at the order. I only need four guards. Besides, there's only going to be one prisoner I'm transporting after a few minutes."

The man shrugged. "In that case, why not?"

* * *

MADDUX SAT IN A dimly lit room for nearly half an hour before he noticed any activity outside. He heard the voices of several men talking on the other side of the door and could see the shadows their legs cast. After a brief discussion, one of the men entered and marched over to Maddux. Hoisting him onto his feet, the guard directed Maddux toward the hallway.

"Will you please tell me what's going on this time?" Maddux pleaded. "Where are you taking me? I need to speak with someone at the U.S. embassy."

The guard chuckled and tightened his grip on Maddux's arm. "Your embassy can't help you, but I can tell you that you're going to be excited about your little trip today."

Maddux furrowed his brow. "Why's that?"

"Because you get to take a ride with your little friend."

"My little friend?"

They rounded the corner, and Maddux noticed Phil standing against the wall in handcuffs along with Beck.

"The three of you are going on a journey tonight," the guard said. "I hope you enjoy it."

He shoved Maddux toward another guard, who checked the cuffs and tightened them one more notch.

"That wasn't necessary," Maddux said as he felt the cuffs now digging into his bones.

The guard smiled and didn't say a word.

"Let's go," one of the other guards directed.

Maddux and the other two prisoners were ushered through a pair of double doors and onto a prison transport vehicle. They all took a seat on one side and were then promptly fastened to the wall—and each other—with a chain-link harness. The guards slapped bindings on the prisoners' feet and secured them to the floor. Then the guards all took their seats opposite of the prisoners.

The truck's engine roared to life, and the vehicle rumbled along slowly.

"What's next?" Maddux whispered to Phil.

Phil, who was seated between Maddux and Beck, shook his head.

"Whatever it is, I can't imagine it being a good situation for any of us. Perhaps they're going to shoot us in the head and bury us out in the middle of nowhere."

"Why not just kill us at The Stasi?"

"They need to make us disappear."

"So maybe we live but spend the rest of our lives in a gulag?"

Phil shook his head. "I can't imagine working in a gulag for the rest of my life to be considered living, but at least there's a chance we might be able to break out of one of those."

"From what I've heard, any escape attempt would be very difficult."

"But at least we'd have a chance to go out on our terms if we failed. Can't ask for more than that."

"I have some friends on the outside, friends in the government," Maddux said. "And if I had a way to communicate, I could request their help. But I doubt that's happening at this point. No one would be willing to risk everything to save me anyway."

"Well, since I'm in here with you, I hope you're wrong—but you're probably right. After all, is there any legitimate reason someone would want to sacrifice their life for yours?"

"You really know how to boost a guy's confidence."

Phil chuckled and looked down.

Maddux did the same. He then threw his head back, resting it against the side of the truck.

They bumped along the road for a few minutes before the vehicle lurched and then skidded to a stop.

The guards all looked at one another confused, and Maddux could tell something wasn't going the way it was supposed to. And that was fine by him.

"Maybe you're getting your wish," he whispered to Phil.

* * *

VOIGT eased into the driver's seat and shot a quick glance over at his traveling companion. The guard assigned to the front seat stared out the opposite window, giving off the not-so-subtle hint that he wasn't interested in small talk.

But Voigt persisted. "I heard on the radio that it's expected to snow tonight."

"I can't remember the last time it snowed in November," the guard said. "That would surprise me."

"I'm not sure anything surprises me any more."

"Well, hopefully our transport this evening doesn't have any surprises."

"That's what I'm counting on," Voigt said.

"Good."

From inside the truck, he heard one of the other guards tap on the wall three times, signaling that they were ready to proceed.

Voigt eyed the man closely, checking out how he held his gun and what his posture said about his readiness. Immobilizing him was going to be critical to the mission's success.

Voigt steered the transport vehicle toward the gate. He handed all his documents to the man in the guard house. After a cursory glance, he returned the papers and raised the gate arm, allowing Voigt to exit The Stasi.

At the designated spot, Voigt flashed his lights.

"What was that for?" the guard in the passenger seat asked.

"What was what for?" Voigt shot back.

"Flashing your lights like that. Why did you do that?"

"I'm just getting familiar with this dashboard. I was trying to find the switch for bright and dim."

They hummed along in silence for a few minutes before the guard got antsy.

"Let me see those papers," he demanded.

Voigt nodded at a folder containing them on the middle seat. "Help yourself."

The guard snatched the folder and started reading. After a moment, he snapped it shut and slapped it down.

"You're going the wrong way," he said. "We need to take care of two of these prisoners first in a designated spot. You're not headed in that direction. You need to turn around right now."

Voigt ignored the man and kept driving.

"I said turn around now," the guard repeated, his

voice growing more intense.

"I know a better way," Voigt said. "I've lived here my whole life."

"That's not the way we go. You're breaking protocol."

Voigt waved off the man. "Would you relax? It's going to be fine."

As Voigt came around the corner, he saw a roadblock in front of them.

"I told you to turn around," the man said.

"I'm sure it's routine and there's nothing to worry about," Voigt snapped.

A man stepped in front of the vehicle's path and held both hands in the air.

Voigt slammed on the brakes, skidding to a stop just a few feet in front of the guard.

MADDUX FURROWED HIS BROW as he looked at Phil. The guards sitting on the other side of the truck also appeared confused at the abrupt stop. Based on the looks on their faces, Maddux realized something was seriously amiss.

"Should we get out and see what's going on?" one of the guards asked in Russian.

"Just sit tight," the head guard said. "We have a new driver tonight. Maybe he made a wrong turn. If anyone can keep him in line, Otto can."

"Maybe it's a new checkpoint," the third guard suggested.

The head guard wagged his finger.

"We would've been informed about that before we left, but this is Berlin. You never know what to expect here."

As the vehicle idled, the seconds turned into minutes. After three minutes, one of the guards sighed.

"Someone should go outside and find out what's happening," he said, appealing to the head guard.

"No," he countered. "We never allow the prisoners to outnumber us. It's a hard rule that we will not violate."

"Fine," the guard said, resigned. "We're probably getting attacked."

"Are you forgetting that we have Otto up front? Everything will be all right."

Maddux was starting to wonder, too. *Are we getting attacked right now? And if so, are we about to be freed?*

Maddux considered volunteering to go with the guard so that they could keep their guard-to-prisoner ratio intact. The curiosity was starting to nag at him. Instead, he chose to appeal to their manhood.

"Look at us," Maddux said in Russian. "Do you really think you can't send someone outside to find out what the delay is all about? This is really starting to make me uncomfortable."

The head guard stood, his head bumping the top of the roof. He towered over Maddux. The guard narrowed his eyes and stooped low, getting eye level with Maddux.

"You think I care about how comfortable you are right now? Or I'm concerned that you are so interested about what's taking place beyond those doors?"

Maddux shrugged. "It seems like you're the only one in the truck who doesn't. And I find that strange."

The guard backhanded Maddux, catching him square across his cheek. Maddux's head snapped to the side, but he refused to show any sign that he was intimidated.

The guard was about to deliver another blow but froze when the back was unlocked. When the doors swung open, a pair of armed East German soldiers were standing there, guns trained on the men inside.

"Get out," one of the guards said in German to the KGB agents.

"It is against our protocol to allow the prisoners to outnumber the guards."

One of the German guards fired his weapon in the air several times. "I don't care what your protocol is. When I tell you to get out, you get out."

"What is this?" the head Russian asked.

"It's a new checkpoint. We heard that someone infiltrated The Stasi, and we're looking for him."

The Russian guard huffed a laugh, almost in disbelief of the news.

"Infiltrated The Stasi? I didn't realize that was even possible."

"A driver was found stashed in the back of his trunk, a driver who was supposed to be on this particular route."

"If that's true, we need to make sure someone is watching these men at all times. This could be some attempt to free a prisoner."

The German guard chuckled as he pointed inside at the prisoners. "I don't see anyone here who appears to be a threat. But why don't we just eliminate the possibility altogether and shoot these men?"

The Russian shook his head. "My superiors would not appreciate that. Some of these men are more valuable alive than dead."

"Very well then. But we will need to do a thorough inspection of the vehicle. And I'm going to need all of the prisoners to exit the vehicle as well."

The Russian guard frowned. "I'm afraid I can't let that happen."

"I'm afraid you don't have a choice," the German said, training his weapon on the Russian.

"Fine. Unlock them."

One of the other Russian guards worked quickly to free the three prisoners from the bindings that kept them tethered to the truck's floor and side. However, he kept them all connected to one another and led them out of the truck and onto the ground.

The guard from the front they called Otto sauntered over to the other Russians.

"We're not going to make our deadline," Otto said.

"Some things are beyond our control."

Otto shook his head. "And some things aren't, like taking the prescribed route. He was taking us the long way, telling me to be quiet because he's lived in Berlin his whole life. I was trying to convince him to return to the route, but he insisted."

"And here we are," the head guard said, "stuck at a stupid German checkpoint. What seems to be the delay now?"

"I'm not sure. There was a lot of yelling and screaming earlier. They wanted to see his papers. I just stayed out of it. You know how these German guards can get."

Maddux strained to look around the corner of the truck to see what was happening near the front. He saw the driver receiving a stern lecture from one of the German guards. Then the guard shoved his rifle into the driver's back and marched him into the wooded area nearby.

"Look at that," one of the Russians remarked, pointing toward the driver.

"What are they doing?" Otto asked.

Before anyone could offer up any plausible explanations, a gunshot ripped through the night. The driver crumpled to the ground. Then another shot.

The German guard stomped out of the woods and strode toward the back of the vehicle.

"You'll need to find a new driver," he announced.

"You can't just shoot him like that?" the head Russian guard protested. "Now we have no driver, not to mention we have to explain this incident to our superiors."

"I'm sure you will think of something, but a thank you might be a good place to start. That man was a spy, and he was planning on sabotaging your mission. He was a traitor."

The guard spun around and trained his weapon on Maddux. "And so is this one."

Maddux swallowed hard. "What do you mean? I've already told you that I'm just someone who works in advertising for Opel cars."

"That's a lie, Mr. Maddux, isn't it? You don't even work for Opel, do you?"

"Of course I do," Maddux said. "How do you even—"

The German guard held up a folder and shook the documents. "I read this," he said. "And I know a phony when I see it, like that driver."

Maddux shook his head. "I swear I'm just an advertising account manager for Opel, nothing more, nothing less."

Otto stepped forward and shook the guard's hand, ending the back-and-forth exchange. "Thank you for your help. We'll take care of this prisoner. We don't want anything to go wrong with this transport—at least, not any more wrong than it has already gone."

Otto turned to look at the rest of the Russians. "I'll be happy to drive, if no one else objects."

"We really need another driver or at least another guard," the head guard warned.

Before the argument went any further, Otto crumpled to the ground.

XXX

MADDUX TRIED TO TURN around to assess the situation. The chains connecting him to Phil prevented a complete scan of the area behind them, but he suspected they were all in danger and needed to take cover. In the midst of the confusion, the other Russian guards crouched low and looked around, glancing toward the woods as they sought protection behind the transport van.

Maddux attempted to follow their lead, tugging on the chain and giving a knowing glance to Phil. Beck didn't protest either, following their lead.

But almost before the chaos started, it ended.

One by one, the Russian guards fell limp onto the ground until all three of them were out cold just like Otto.

Maddux looked over at the bodies strewn near the edge of the road, wondering if he was about to be next. He turned to search for the German guards, who were storming toward them, weapons held at their sides.

"You guys ready to get the hell outta here?" one of the German guards asked in English.

Maddux studied the man intently, still trying to make sense of the comment. It wasn't until he saw the other guard that he felt at ease.

Rose removed her hat as her long brown locks fell around her shoulders. With a wink, she smiled at Maddux.

"Didn't think we were coming, did you?" she asked.

Maddux's jaw was agape as he tried to process what had just happened through a new lens.

Another man came bounding over the fence out of the woods.

"Meet Günter Voigt, your driver," Rose said, gesturing toward him.

Voigt forced a smile and turned toward one of the other guards. "That was a little too believable, don't you think?"

The guard chuckled. "I had to sell it. They'll still be scratching their heads for days when they wake up."

Rose introduced Bull and Darby to Maddux, who then introduced his fellow prisoners, Phil and Beck.

"That was quite a production," Maddux said. "I can't believe Pritchett sanctioned something like this."

Rose laughed nervously. "He didn't. And we're not home yet, so we need to get moving."

"What are we going to do with these KGB stooges?" Bull asked.

"I'm open for suggestions as long as it doesn't involve killing them," Rose said. "The last thing we want is to turn this into an international incident."

"Didn't they already make it one?" Darby asked.

"I'm not here to debate that," she said, glancing at her watch. "Let's just get them into the back of this transport van, park it a few miles into the woods, and get going."

Bull unlocked the prisoners before placing them in the back of the van and securing them to the side and floor.

"How long are they going to be out?" Maddux asked. "If they wake up any time soon—"

"They'll be out long enough," Rose said.

"Long enough for what?"

"Long enough for us to get back across the border."

Maddux looked around at the party that now numbered six.

"This is a large group to get across the border."

Rose smiled as she strode toward the front of the transport vehicle. "Bull and Darby are agents here in East Berlin, but we're taking back more than this."

"How in the world do you propose to do that in such a timely manner? You didn't reconfigure a bus that could hide us all, did you?"

Rose shot a sideways glance at Voigt. "You wanna tell them?"

He shrugged. "Why don't you do the honors?"

"You sure? It's your idea," she said.

Maddux scowled. "Would someone just tell me what the plan is?"

"Fine. I'll tell them since it's my idea," Voigt said as he climbed into the van. He turned the ignition, and the engine roared to life.

Maddux hustled around the front to the driver's side. "Well, what are you waiting on?"

Voigt smiled wryly. "We're going to steal a train."

XXXI

AFTER STRANDING THE PRISON transport van, Maddux piled into Bull's car along with Rose, Beck, and Phil. Darby volunteered to drive Voigt back to his home where he could collect his family and then rendezvous with the rest of the team at the location where the heist was set to occur.

"Are you out of your mind?" Maddux asked Rose, whose grin hadn't vanished from her face since successfully retrieving him.

"I must say that it's so fun to see your work in action in the field," she said, brushing off his rhetorical question. "I mean, I've tested these little tranquilizer gadgets before, but I didn't realize they were so effective. You don't even have to be that accurate with them. Pretty much any solid strike to a person's flesh will do the trick."

Maddux's eyes widened, and he cocked his head as he stared at her. "Do you realize that what you just did could've gone wrong—very wrong?"

Rose tousled Maddux's hair. "Of course I do. But nothing went wrong. It was a stroke of brilliance."

Maddux sighed. "Do I need to remind you that

extracting someone isn't the real challenge here? It's getting people out of the country that presents the biggest obstacle."

"I'm very well aware of that," Rose said. "We wouldn't be here if you had been able to conquer it yourself."

She gave him a coy wink, but the gesture only annoyed Maddux. He didn't understand her motivating factors for taking such risks.

"But why do it? Why risk everything, even your life?"

"Pritchett was too wound up about it all. He was paralyzed by his own fear. Somebody had to do something, and he wasn't about to do a damn thing because he doesn't trust anyone."

"I don't know if that's the ultimate brownnosing job or career suicide."

She slapped Maddux on his knee. "Well, it doesn't matter now because it's done."

"It's not done yet. The last I checked, we're still in East Germany. We need to get across that border to consider this a success. Even I wasn't able to get Dr. Schwarz out. Besides, shouldn't he be the reason you're doing this anyway?"

"He is. And he's exactly where you left him. All we need to do is swing by and snag him before we get back to West Germany."

Maddux closed his eyes and exhaled slowly. "And you're going to do all this by stealing a train?"

She chuckled. "Sounds crazy, I know. But I think this is going to work."

"When we have the lives of this many people in

our hands, we need to deal in absolutes. We have to *know* this is going to work."

"Come on, Ed. You know by now that we never really *know* if anything is going to work. It's all educated guesses. And while unconventional, this plan should work."

Maddux closed his eyes and shook his head. "How did you even come up with this?"

"I didn't exactly come up with this on my own. Günter Voigt is the one who suggested it."

"Voigt? The guy who double crossed us?"

"And also just helped you escape from KGB custody. Don't be so quick to judge."

"You trust him?"

"Voigt used to be a train engineer here before the KGB pressed him into service. He didn't really have a choice. Now, he just wants his family and his life back. If he isn't sincere, he has fooled me completely."

Bull, who had remained quiet the entire drive, finally piped up. "And he will have fooled me too, but I doubt that's the case," Bull said. "I believe he's about as sincere of a person as I've ever met—and someone who cares deeply about getting his family to a country where they won't be monitored every waking hour."

"Did you know him before Rose came to town?"

Bull shook his head. "Not exactly, but I have been able to glean that from him during the short time that I've known him."

"Are you a hundred percent sure that his desire is to get his family out of East Germany and somewhere safe?" Maddux asked.

Bull nodded. "Without a single doubt."

"In that case, I'll go along with it," Maddux said. "You and Rose couldn't both be wrong, could you?"

Rose patted Maddux's knee again. "It's going to be all right," she whispered.

* * *

MADDUX KNOCKED ON the door to the safe house and waited for Schwarz to answer. After a few seconds, approaching footsteps were followed by a question.

"Yes?" Schwarz asked.

"Rockets to nowhere," Maddux said.

Silence.

"You know who this is," Maddux said. "Time to go."

Still no response.

"This isn't a game. We're leaving now, and I know you don't want to stay here forever."

The latch clicked, and the door opened just enough for Schwarz to look out and see Maddux.

"I changed the password when Rose came by," he said. "I just had to be sure it was you."

"Thank you for staying put. But we have to move now."

"We're going home?"

"God willing, we're all going home tonight."

Maddux led Schwarz down a back stairwell, which exited into an alley where Bull was waiting for them. With the rest of the team preparing for the heist, Bull volunteered to drive since he was more familiar with the city and the East German secret police's observation practices.

"How are we going to get across the border?" Schwarz asked. "Am I going to be stuffed into a trunk?"

"We're going a little less conventional tonight," Maddux said.

"Hot air balloon?"

"We're going to take a train—literally."

* * *

A MILE WEST of the Albrechtshof train station, Rose and Darby worked with Phil and Beck to set up the heist, while waiting on the rest of the team to join them. The plan to overtake the train was relatively simple, but they needed everyone doing their part in order to pull it off.

They had just finished going over the different roles everyone was to play when Bull and Maddux arrived with Schwarz. Rose greeted them and shook the doctor's hand.

"I told you we'd come get you," Rose said.

Schwarz looked up and down the track. "I'm not going to celebrate until we're on the other side. I've heard too many stories."

Rose checked her watch. They had ten minutes before the 11:55 Albrechtshof train made its final run of the night.

"Where's Voigt?" Maddux asked. "Since this is his brainchild, don't you need him here?"

Rose strained to see down the road, peering into the darkness. "He's the engineer, the only one who knows how to make this train move. Without him, this plan is dead."

"And do you have a backup plan?" Schwarz asked, his eyes widening.

"It's a little too late for that," she said. "It's all or nothing."

Maddux cursed under his breath. "I knew we should've never trusted him."

XXXII

VOIGT HUSTLED UP THE STEPS to his apartment, taking them two at a time. After unlocking the door, he slipped inside and rushed to the back to check on Sigrid and his children. He noticed all their bags packed and lined up neatly in the hallway as he breezed down it.

"Is that you, Günter?" Sigrid asked.

"Coming, *schatzi*," he said.

When he entered the room, he found the secret police agents grimacing and struggling with their bindings. They growled and grunted to no avail.

"It's time to go," Voigt said. "Let's secure this door and get out of here."

She scrambled to her feet and handed the weapon to her husband. "I was beginning to wonder if you were coming back because if you hadn't—"

Voigt put his arm around Sigrid. "Let's not think about what could've been, okay? I'm here, and all we have to do is make it to the rendezvous point on foot in the next fifteen minutes."

Her eyes widened. "You think we can do that with the children? Stefan and Petra have usually been in bed for several hours now. It's nearly midnight."

"We don't have any other options. There's really only one way to find out, and I don't want to waste any more time dealing in hypotheticals. Let's run and prove that we can do it. I say we can do it with time to spare."

"Stefan, Petra," Sigrid called.

The two children appeared in the hallway, standing attentively against the wall.

"Yes, Mother," Stefan said.

"You each need to pick up your bag and follow us," Sigrid said. "We're going on a little adventure, but it won't happen if you don't keep up. In fact, we might face dreadful consequences."

"Does it have anything to do with those men who came to our house?" Petra asked.

"Don't you worry about that," Sigrid said, placing her hand on Petra's shoulders. "Everybody makes their own decisions and suffers the consequences of them—or revels in the outcome. It all depends on which path you choose and which fate awaits you."

Voigt snapped his fingers. "Enough with the philosophy lesson. We need to move now."

He spun and headed toward the door, snagging his suitcase on the way. Voigt stopped and looked behind him to make sure everyone was rushing out the door with him.

"Everyone ready?"

Petra and Stefan held up their bags. Sigrid nodded as a tear trickled down her cheek.

"There will be a time for tears later," Voigt said. "I will miss this place too, but you must know the life we've always dreamed of is waiting for us just beyond that wall."

She sniffled and nodded, her lips quivering. Opening her mouth to speak, she stopped and wiped teardrops from the corners of her eyes with her hands.

"We don't have any time to waste," he said, placing his hand on her shoulder and ushering her toward the door.

A trio of knocks startled Voigt, arresting his attention.

"Who could that be at this time of night?" Sigrid whispered.

Voigt placed his hand out in a calming gesture.

"Just relax. I'll handle it." Voigt took a deep breath and turned the knob, cracking the door open just a few inches.

"Yes," Voigt said as he recognized his neighbor Felix Ludwig standing in the hallway.

"Good evening, Günter."

"It's late, Felix. What could you possibly want that couldn't wait until morning?"

"I've noticed some strange activity taking place here today," Ludwig said. "I wanted to stop by and check in on what's been happening."

"It must be your imagination. I suggest you go back to your apartment and leave us alone. I don't want my children to be awakened by your visit at this time of night."

"I'm sorry, but this can't wait. I need some proof that what I observed earlier isn't happening."

Voigt cocked his head to one side. "What exactly do you think is happening?"

"People are going into your apartment, but they aren't coming out. That's a little strange, don't you think?"

"Was it men?" Voigt asked. "I've had my suspicions about Sigrid."

The effort to deflect the accusations was a valiant one, but it wasn't enough to redirect Ludwig.

"I know a gentleman caller when I see one. That wasn't the case tonight. These were government agents, secret police and the like searching for something. But these people never left. One by one, they entered your apartment. And for all I know, they're still in there. Perhaps even dead."

Voigt maintained his firm grip on the knob and slid his foot against the bottom side of the door to prevent a sudden effort to get inside by Ludwig that would reveal the truth. Shoring up his defenses proved to be a wise one as Ludwig put his shoulder into the door but went nowhere.

Ludwig looked up at Voigt and glared at him.

"What is it that you're hiding in there?" Ludwig asked.

"Go to bed, Felix. It's late, and I don't want anyone to wake up."

"Why such an evasive response? You still haven't told me what—or who—you're hiding in your apartment."

"And you haven't told me who is hiding in yours," Voigt fired back. "See, we're even. Now, please, leave us alone."

Instead of complying, Ludwig shoved his hand through the small gap in the door and poked Voigt in the eyes. Instinctively, Voigt put his hands to his face and pivoted to bend over. That was all Ludwig needed to shove his way inside and find Voigt's family standing there with their bags.

"I knew it," Ludwig said. "You're leaving under the cover of night. What happened to those people who visited earlier but never left your apartment?"

Voigt stood upright and glared at Ludwig. "I suggest you turn around and go back to your apartment before you make me do something that I absolutely will not regret."

Ludwig laughed. "You couldn't hurt a flea, Günter. Now I'm going to find out what happened."

Ludwig turned his back on Voigt and started walking down the hallway. Voigt took his wife by the shoulders and looked into her eyes.

"Go two blocks west of the Albrechtshof station," Voigt said. "I'll meet you there."

He kissed her on the forehead.

"Hurry, Günter," she said. "I don't want to be apart any longer."

He nodded knowingly and dashed down the hall toward the room where Ludwig was scrambling to open the door.

XXXIII

MADDUX PACED AROUND in circles, stopping only briefly to look down the empty street for a silhouetted figure charging toward them. He cupped his hands and breathed on them in an effort to stay warm. As he did, he noticed a snowflake flit toward the ground.

"Did you know there was snow in the forecast?" he said as he looked over at Rose.

"This entire night has been stormy enough without the weather," she said. "What's one more obstacle for us to escape this place?"

"If the track gets icy enough, the engineer won't be able to stop the train even if he wanted to."

"Then pray for a warm spell," she said.

Bull joined them, crossing his arms and rubbing them to stay warm. "Is Günter really going to show up?"

Rose sighed and shook her head. "I just don't know."

"This is your operation. What does your gut tell you?"

"My gut tells me that I feel sick right now," she said. "I dragged everyone into this operation, and if it fails—"

"It's not going to fail," Maddux said. "We'll make it work without him."

"But he knew all the details."

"What details?" Bull asked.

"Where to pull the switch for the tracks to send us crashing into the wall and into West Germany."

"Maybe we can figure it out," Maddux said. "Does anyone have a map?"

Bull nodded and produced one from his back pocket. "It's a must if you live here," he said. "You don't want to find yourself in places you shouldn't be, even if by mistake."

Maddux and Bull studied the map for a couple minutes before agreeing on two possible locations for the switch.

"We have an educated guess," Maddux said.

Rose shot an eyebrow upward. "An educated guess? I didn't think you were a big fan of those."

"Touché," he said. "I'll let you roast me later for my hypocrisy, but in the interest of time, please bear with us."

Maddux explained why the two locations were the most likely to have a switch near the border. Bull added that he was reasonably sure he'd seen track veering toward the wall near one of those locations.

"Let's hope you're right," she said, handing the map back to Bull. "In the meantime, we need to get that car up onto the tracks."

Based on Rose's timepiece, she announced the train was due to arrive within the next five minutes. Along with Rose, Maddux hustled over to the vehicle they'd stolen from the street. He watched Rose turn her back against the bumper and push along with the rest of the men until the car came to rest across the tracks.

A wry grin spread across Maddux's face. He shook his head as he stared at her.

"What?" she asked. "Haven't you ever seen a woman push a car onto railroad tracks before?"

Maddux laughed. "You have more spunk than anyone I've ever met."

"At this point, I'll take that as a compliment, *Mr. Whittaker*."

Maddux turned and looked down the road and saw a few figures emerging from the darkness. They were all carrying bags and running.

He tapped Rose on the shoulder and pointed down the street. "Were you expecting them?"

After a few more seconds, the silhouettes took shape—a woman and two children.

"It's Voigt's family," Rose said.

"Then where's Voigt?" Maddux asked.

A train whistle sounded in the distance.

"We don't have time to worry about that now," she said. "It's show time."

* * *

ROSE RACED TOWARD the car and propped up the hood. She struck a match and dropped it into a small bucket loaded with straw and paper, giving the illusion that her vehicle was smoking. Positioning herself near the trunk, she began waving a white handkerchief in an attempt to alert the engineer to her situation before it was too late.

The engineer stuck his head out the side window and reacted quickly, throwing on the brakes to his steam engine. The train hissed as the wheels ground to a halt, the nose coming to rest only a few meters away from the side of the car.

"What happened out there?" the engineer asked, shouting from the window.

Rose didn't say anything, instead marching up to the ladder and climbing aboard.

"I'm afraid we need to commandeer this train," she said.

"You need to do what?" he asked, his brow furrowed. "And since when did they let women into the military?"

Bull slammed the butt of his rifle into the engineer's head, knocking him out cold. The coal stoker raised both hands in a gesture of surrender and stepped backward.

"You're a smart man," Bull said to the stoker. "Go have a seat."

Rose signaled to Darby, Schwarz, and Maddux to shove the car off the tracks so they could get going. She was watching them work when she heard a woman's voice, one that was familiar.

"Rose," said the woman. "It's me, Sigrid Voigt."

Rose looked out the engine window and saw Voigt's wife with her two children in tow.

"Come aboard quickly," Rose said. "We need to get going."

"What about my husband?" Sigrid asked.

"What about him? Why isn't he here?"

Sigrid shook her head. "We had a neighbor causing us trouble. He said he'd take care of it and meet us here quickly."

Rose looked down the street in the direction Sigrid and her children had come from. There was still no sign of Voigt.

"I'm sorry, Sigrid, but we can't wait any longer or else this entire mission is in jeopardy. There are people here who I have to get across the border tonight, and there isn't time to wait."

Tears streamed down Sigrid's face.

"I don't know what to do," she said between sobs.

"I believe your husband is a good man," Rose said. "And I think everything he did was to give you and your children a better life. If you don't take this chance, you will most likely spend the rest of your days regretting it. I think I know he'd want you to take it."

"But what good is a better life if it's apart from him?"

Rose glanced ahead on the tracks to see that the vehicle had been cleared and the men were sprinting toward the train. "If you stay here, you won't be spending your life together. He will be blamed for this, and you will be a widow living in this horrible place. I know that may sound callous, but you need the straight truth right now because if you don't make a decision, one will be made for you since we're leaving now."

Rose looked at Bull and nodded.

Bull released the brakes as the train's wheels started to slowly turn.

Sigrid hoisted her children onto the train and scrambled up after them.

The train chugged along slowly until it resumed its speed.

"What if I'm wrong about where the switch is?" Bull asked as he looked at Rose.

"We're all in at this point. The stakes were decided a long time ago."

Maddux climbed into the engineer cab, joining Rose and Bull.

"Is Darby keeping an eye on Schwarz?" she asked.

Maddux nodded. "You sure the guards aren't going to open fire on us once we roll through Albrechtshof station?"

"I'm not sure of anything at this point except than I'm going to get over that wall tonight with you and Dr. Schwarz and Voigt's family one way or another. But brace yourself because we're coming up on the station in less than thirty seconds."

The train chugged along, continuing to gain speed. She stuck her head out of the side to breathe in the cool, fresh air. Since they had taken over the train, the snowfall had transitioned from flurries to heavy, wet flakes.

Rose peeked around the bend as the tracks started to curve. The station was dead ahead, and the platform attendants acted bewildered by the train's approaching speed. One man ran forward and waved his arms in an effort to get it to stop. But Rose ignored him.

Seconds later, they were zipping through the station. The guards who were milling around seemed shocked by the train's failure to stop but didn't take any action to go after it.

"Looks like they didn't know what hit them," Rose said to Maddux.

Maddux flashed a brief smile that vanished almost as quickly as it had appeared. "We're not out of the woods yet," he said. "We'll be at one of the switch locations in less than two minutes."

"How far is the one after that?" she asked.

"Maybe another mile at the most. But we need to

start slowing down if we're going to change the tracks."

"Once you make the switch, how much track will I have before we smash into the wall?"

"Bull estimated about half a mile, if that. It should be enough for us to generate sufficient speed but not enough time for the East Germans to take any measures to stop us if they suspect anything."

Rose poked her head outside the cab window again and looked behind the train.

"It's hard to tell if they're panicking now or not. But I don't see a flurry of activity, that's for sure."

"It is almost midnight," Maddux said.

They clicked along the tracks for another minute before Rose nodded at Maddux, giving him the sign to yank on the brake handle. The train began to slow, but not quickly enough. He looked over at Bull.

"Can you give me a hand here?" Maddux asked.

Bull rushed over, and the two men applied pressure on the handle. The engine slowed, but not in time for anyone to get out and make an attempt at throwing the switch.

"Hold on," Rose said. "We got lucky. That wasn't the switch."

Maddux stood upright. "I'm not sure I'd call that luck yet. If this next one isn't the switch, we're in big trouble."

"Just be ready," she said. "We won't stoke the coals until after the switch, and we'll start the brake earlier."

"This whole thing would've been much easier if you just had a gadget that could safely vault us over the wall."

"You know I've already thought about that, don't you?"

"I figured as much."

They chugged along, slowing down much earlier as they approached the second potential location for the switch. Maddux leaned out the cab window to get a peek.

"Have a look," he said.

Rose stood on her tiptoes and craned her neck to see. The track curved to the left, but there was a segment that appeared to veer right just as it straightened back out again.

"That's gotta be it," she said.

"This switch has to be smooth," Bull said. "We have company."

"What do you mean?" Rose asked.

"From what I can tell, I think there are some East German soldiers who control a train and are chasing us," he said.

"In other words, we can't back up if we miss it," Rose said.

"Exactly."

Rose stuck her head out again and strained to see where the tracks diverged. She had slowed the train to a crawl in an effort to make sure they hit the switch. But when she poked her head out again, she furrowed her brow at the scene unfolding in the distance.

"What is that?" she asked aloud, tapping Maddux on the shoulder.

She eased out of the way so Maddux could look. When he retreated back inside the cab, his eyes were wide.

"I think that's Voigt trying to pull the switch for us."

As they neared the location, the man Maddux believed to be Voigt was shouting something.

"What?" Maddux called back.

"It won't budge," Voigt said.

Maddux jumped out of the cab.

"What are you doing?" Rose asked.

"He said it won't budge," Maddux called back over his shoulder as he raced to lend a hand.

Rose watched Maddux slide into the dirt and grab the switch, tugging on it in concert with Voigt. She then looked behind them.

The trailing locomotive was bearing down on them.

XXXIV

MADDUX JAMMED HIS FEET up against one of the railroad ties and yanked hard on the lever. Years of disuse resulted in a rusty device that wasn't complying with their request to shift positions. Maddux took a deep breath, adjusted his grip, and pulled again.

"Come on," Maddux said.

"I don't think it's going to move," Voigt said.

"I didn't think you were going to come back, but here you are. So, let's think positive, okay?"

Voigt nodded, and the two men repositioned themselves to make another run at changing the tracks. The train was crawling along, but the real problem lurked farther down the line where another engine was charging up behind them.

"Now," Maddux said.

He strained every muscle he knew he had—and some he wasn't even aware existed. For a second, the rusted metal moved a smidge, but not nearly enough to redirect the oncoming locomotive in a different direction entirely.

"We can't quit," Maddux said. "This is it."

He paused and looked at Voigt, who stood to the

right and was trying to get a good grip on the handle.

"For your family," Maddux said. "For Sigrid and Petra and Stefan."

"For freedom," Voigt said.

On the count of three, both men pulled hard. Maddux felt the veins in his neck bulging as he applied maximum pressure on the lever. Suddenly, the switch started to move—and far more than just an inch. After a few seconds of constant pressure, Maddux nearly lost his balance as he pulled the bar all the way to the ground, changing the direction of the track.

Maddux clambered to his feet before hugging Voigt in celebration. They both wore wide grins as they reveled in their victory.

The train eased onto that area of the track, sending it chugging straight toward the wall.

"Change it back," Rose shouted.

Maddux glanced behind Rose's train and saw the German soldiers gaining momentum.

"Did she say what I think she just said?" Voigt asked.

Maddux nodded. "Get ready to do this again."

As soon as the train passed, Maddux estimated they had less than thirty seconds to get the job completed. Working in tandem again with Voigt, the two men snatched the lever and started to push it back to its original position. The switch remained stubborn.

Maddux glanced up to see the other train closing in. He estimated they had maybe ten seconds at best.

"For freedom," Maddux said with a grunt as he worked the switch.

"For freedom," Voigt said.

Then the switch surrendered, giving up its fight with barely a whimper. The metal clanked hard against the rocks as it returned to the exclusive East German route.

Maddux grabbed Voigt's hand, snatching him to his feet and in the direction of the train Rose was now guiding. Both men stumbled for a second before they began to pick up speed. The guards from the trailing train fired at them, peppering shots all around them, but none of them were able to hit their mark.

The train's eighth and final car was reserved for passengers. But Maddux just wanted to be near the back when it made impact with the wall. According to Bull's earlier estimate, the ride wouldn't last long.

Maddux's train picked up speed, while soldiers hopped off their train and gave chase on foot. Maddux gritted his teeth and raced toward the final car. Following several attempts, Maddux grabbed the railing and pulled himself up to safety. He turned around to help Voigt, who was struggling to keep up—and then a bullet tore through his shoulder.

For a few seconds, Maddux watched Voigt slow down, as if he'd resigned himself to the fact that he couldn't make it. The train had started to edge away from him, while the German guards were gaining ground. All he had needed to do was grip the rear rail and hold on until someone could help him gain his bearings and climb aboard. But that task was easier said than done, especially for a man with a bleeding shoulder. The pain, the blood, the hopelessness—all of it appeared to be having an effect on Voigt at the worst possible moment.

Maddux stepped inside the train and hollered for Sigrid to come help her husband. She dashed down the aisle and onto the platform at the rear of the car, urging him to continue.

"You can do it," she said. "I know you can. Keep running."

Maddux looked up to see the wall fast approaching. He estimated they'd be there in twenty-five seconds, thirty tops. But it'd seem like a hollow victory if the man who'd concocted a way out of the country didn't get the chance of freedom with his family.

"Come on, Voigt," Maddux said. "Keep running. You can make it."

Voigt lunged toward Maddux and grabbed his right forearm. The grip almost immediately started to slip. Seconds later, Voigt couldn't hold it and his hand fell free.

"Use both hands this time to grab onto me," Maddux said. "I'll get you aboard."

Voigt pumped both arms as he tried to keep up with the train. As he edged within an arms' length, he reached out again.

"If I don't make it, disable the emergency brake," Voigt yelled.

"You're going to make it."

"Just promise me you will."

"I promise. Now give me your hand." Maddux stretched as far as he could, making contact with Voigt's fingertips. "Almost there."

Then Voigt fell, tumbling onto the ground as a bullet grazed his leg. Maddux watched the scene unfold as German guards on foot about a hundred meters behind raced toward Voigt.

"Get up and keep going," Maddux yelled as the train began picking up speed.

But Voigt didn't move.

XXXV

MADDUX WORMED HIS WAY back inside the caboose, keeping his head down as the Germans continued to fire on the train. He glanced at the passengers who had unwittingly been aboard when the heist and escape plan was hatched. Worried lines marked their foreheads, mothers pulling their children tight. Bullets peppered the side of the car, occasionally shattering glass. Several shards had sliced up Maddux's forearms as he crawled back toward the engine.

The first time Maddux ran through the cars, he hadn't even taken notice of any of the other passengers. But this time, he counted about a dozen people, most wearing worried expressions. Everyone was either lying on the floor beneath the benches or hunched over in their seats, heads down.

To the few who were still sitting, Maddux urged them all to get on the floor. If they were in their seats when the train made contact with the wall, they would likely get tossed around, possibly even thrown outside. All of them complied except one stocky man who eyed Maddux cautiously. He ignored the man as a stubborn fool and kept working his way toward the front.

When he arrived there, he found Bull and the coal stoker working together to heat up the steam engine, while Rose eyed the track ahead.

"How much longer to impact?" Maddux asked.

"About two more minutes," Rose said. "Were you able to get Voigt aboard?"

Maddux shook his head. "I tried, but I couldn't reach him. Then he got shot. But he told me to disable passenger braking."

"Yeah, we talked about that while we were planning this escape. We didn't want anyone to sabotage this."

"Do I need to do this in every car?" he asked.

"Only the ones that contain passengers we didn't bring ourselves."

"They're all concentrated at the car in the back."

"Good," she said. "Just unlink the chain so when it's pulled it won't activate the brakes up here. We're still not going fast enough yet to crash through the wall."

Maddux spun around and hustled toward the car. As he did, he noticed the stocky man standing up and reaching for the brake chain.

Maddux dove headlong into the man's chest, driving him backward. But the man spun, throwing Maddux aside. As Maddux regained his wits, he looked up to see the man dashing toward the chain. Maddux lunged toward the man's feet, tripping him up. This time, Maddux didn't let the man get away, yanking on his legs and reeling him in.

The man turned around and threw a punch toward Maddux, who blocked it with both his hands. Maddux dished out several body blows before a final punch to the face knocked the man out.

With the threat neutralized, Maddux looked up to see an elderly woman hobbling toward the brake chain. He rushed toward her and grabbed her arm just before she could pull.

"That wouldn't be a good idea," he said. "Why don't you lie back down beneath your seat?"

The woman glared at Maddux. "You're going to get us all killed."

"You're going to get your freedom."

"I don't care about my freedom. I just want to go home."

Maddux turned around and disconnected the chain, disabling it from being pulled by any other passengers with an eye on being a hero.

He raced back toward the cab and reported that he'd successfully disabled the brake.

"Anything else I need to do?" he asked.

"Just pray," Rose said. "Thirty more seconds."

Maddux peered out of the cab window and saw the wall fast approaching.

"We need to get back to one of the passenger cars," he said. "You don't want to be up here when we make impact."

"I have to make sure that we don't lose any speed," Rose said.

"We're going plenty fast," Maddux said. He glanced over at the coal stoker. "Isn't that right, mister coal man?"

The stoker nodded.

"See?" Maddux said. "Now get somewhere safe so we can survive this collision. You, too, Bull."

Bull didn't need to be told twice as he hustled out

of the cab. Rose lingered for a moment, checking all the controls.

"Come on, Rose," Maddux said. "This isn't a debate. You're not the captain of a sinking ship."

He put his hand on her, gently pulling her back. She recoiled.

"I just want to make sure we make it through."

Maddux tugged on her arm again. "Everything is set in motion now. The only thing you can do is get into another car to safely await the impact. Now, please don't make me drag you back there."

"Fine," she said. "I'll go."

She shoveled another scoop of coal into the furnace before latching it shut.

"Now," he said.

Rose secured the shovel before hustling out of the cab and through one empty passenger car until she reached an area deemed to be safe.

Maddux found an open spot beneath one of the benches and ushered Rose in first. Behind him, he heard sniffling from Sigrid Voigt. He turned to see her dabbing the corners of her eyes with a handkerchief. He figured she was grappling with the idea that her husband wasn't aboard and was likely dead.

"How long before we collide with the wall?" Maddux asked.

"Fifteen seconds," Rose said.

Maddux counted down in his mind, descending to the number four before the locomotive engine slammed into the wall. While Maddux wasn't sure what to expect, he certainly believed there would be some type of a fiery explosion. Instead, the sound was more reminiscent of a wrecking ball smashing into an old building. Steel twisted and moaned as the train collided with cement. The wall crumbled several meters on each side of engine, which didn't stop until it had fully penetrated the border.

The engine boiler erupted into flames as the engine finally came to rest on its side, while the rest of the train's cars remained upright. Once the motion stopped, the passengers slowly crawled out from underneath their seats. They wore confused looks as they scanned the carnage and exited.

Maddux scrambled to his feet and peered behind them. "The East Germans will be here any minute and we're still not over the border," he said, offering his hand to Rose. "We need to hurry."

Rose stood and scanned the car. "Where's Dr. Schwarz?"

"I'm right here," Schwarz said, raising his hand as he struggled to get upright.

"Exit to the right," Maddux said. "The engine is on fire. It fell on its left side. There's plenty of room to climb over the rubble and get across the line."

Maddux stood outside, assisting everyone onto the ground and through a makeshift path in the wall. He watched as the other train carrying East Germans chugged along the track toward the wall. In the distance, he also noticed several military vehicles speeding toward his position.

"Is anyone else on board?" he called out.

"We're still here," said a woman.

Maddux stuck his head inside and saw Sigrid Voigt, struggling to get Petra and Stefan to their feet. Dashing back inside, Maddux scooped up the two children and raced back toward the door. He glanced over his shoulder at Sigrid, who hadn't moved. Rigid and sullen, she worked over the handkerchief she was holding.

"Sigrid, we have no time. You must come now."

"I—I don't know if I can, not now. Günter is gone. What difference does it make any more?"

Maddux looked at Petra and Stefan. "It will make a world of difference to these two little ones you still have. All is not lost. We can talk about it more later, when we're over the line and we have both time and freedom."

She shook her head. "No, I don't think I can do it—not alone anyway."

"Sigrid, listen to me. They're going to kill you if you don't hurry. Don't let them have the pleasure."

She remained stiff, unmoved by Maddux's plea.

"Mommy, are we going to die?" Petra asked.

The innocent question snapped Sigrid out of her self-loathing. She looked up and shook her head. "Not today, *mäuschen*," Sigrid said. "Not today."

She sprinted toward the door. Maddux didn't waste another second, jumping to the ground and carrying both children with him over the rubble. He heard Sigrid singing a German lullaby right behind him as they ran.

"Don't stop," Maddux said as he approached the rest of the passengers, who had gathered together and were watching the engine burn.

"Why?" one of the men asked. "We're free."

"There are soldiers converging on us, and you're a fool if you don't think they won't start shooting at us until allied troops arrive. Now, run."

No one in the group needed to be told again. They all raced toward a large structure several hundred meters away.

Maddux surveyed the small group, accounting for everyone on board that he knew, except one.

"Phil? Where are you?" Maddux called, his eyes searching through the darkness.

There was no response.

"Phil?" Maddux shouted again. "Phil?"

Nothing.

For a fleeting moment, Maddux considered running back to the train as he tried to calculate if he'd have enough time to search the passenger car for his friend. Maddux called over Bull and Darby and handed them Petra and Stefan. He instructed them to carry them to safety.

"What are you doing?" Rose asked.

"It's Phil," Maddux said. "He didn't make it out. He's probably still on board, lying there unconscious or something like that."

He turned to go, but Rose tugged on his jacket.

"You can't go," she protested. "It's a suicide mission. You'll never make it."

"Those soldiers are going to kill him if I don't help him."

"They're going to kill you too if you do," she said. "You know you don't have enough time. Don't try to be a hero on a mission destined to fail."

Maddux let out an exasperated sigh. He knew she was right. In his rush to get everyone off the train, he'd forgotten to search the car for Phil. Maddux knew he'd never forgive himself for such an error, the disappointment written all over his face.

"Don't," she said. "Don't beat yourself up about it. You did a good thing today. None of these people would be free if it weren't for you."

"But I should've checked. I just—"

"Let it go," she said. "We can debrief later. Let's keep moving, okay?"

Maddux nodded and took Rose's hand. After a few steps, they released each other's hands, breaking into a full sprint. They didn't stop until they rounded the corner of the building. Maddux peered at the engine now fully engulfed in flames. Several East German guards walked over the debris that was once part of the wall. In the distance, he heard a single shot ring out.

Maddux couldn't hold back his tears.

XXXVI

U.S. MILITARY VEHICLES SKIDDED to a stop nearby as they rushed over to the train to inspect the damage. One fire truck rolled onto the scene, and workers began dousing the flaming locomotive. A few soldiers approached the group of passengers and assessed the situation and gathered information about what exactly had happened.

Maddux and Rose explained who they were and gave them Pritchett's name and number. The soldier interviewing them instructed one of his assistants to verify that information with one of his superiors.

While Maddux was still going over all the details with one of the soldiers, a commotion near the train arrested everyone's attention. A man wearing an East German military uniform limped across the line, raising his hand in the air in a gesture of surrender—only one of them fully extended.

"Hold on a second," Maddux said as he strained to see what was happening.

"Do you know him?" the soldier asked.

Maddux shrugged. "I'm not sure. I need to get a closer look. Can we go over there?"

The soldier agreed and accompanied Maddux and Rose as they strode back toward the wreckage near the wall. As they grew nearer, a smile spread across Maddux's face.

"Can you tell now if that's someone you know?" the soldier asked again.

Maddux nodded. "That's one of our assets, the guy who hatched this plot and made it happen."

The soldier whistled and flashed a thumbs up to the commanding officer standing near the man who had just crossed over.

"What's his name?" the soldier asked.

"That's Günter Voigt."

* * *

AFTER VOIGT WAS briefly interviewed by a couple U.S. military personnel, Maddux led him over to Sigrid. She was still huddled up with Petra and Stefan, all softly sobbing.

"There's someone you need to see," Maddux said.

Head down, Sigrid refused to look up. "Can it wait?"

"I don't think you'd want it to."

She looked up and saw her husband. "Günter, we thought you were dead."

"Daddy!" cried Petra and Stefan in unison.

"I'll leave you four alone," Maddux said.

Voigt glanced over his shoulder and mouthed the words thank you to Maddux.

He walked back toward Rose and was only a few meters away when a helicopter hovering overhead arrested everyone's attention.

A U.S. general eased onto the ground and marched

over to the commanding officer. He pointed in the direction of Dr. Schwarz. Immediately, two soldiers hustled over to him and escorted him onto the helicopter. Maddux and Rose watched as the aircraft lifted off the ground and flew away.

"What was that all about?" Maddux asked one of the guards who had led Schwarz to the chopper.

"President's orders," he said as he ran past.

Maddux looked at Rose. "Someone is going to get some medals for all of this."

She shook her head. "Just doing my job, right?"

Maddux chuckled. "Your job is to make gadgets that help agents in the field, not lead audacious—and unsanctioned, mind you—missions behind enemy lines."

"Yet, here I am."

"Here you are," Maddux said with a smile. "You know Pritchett is going to kill you?"

"Is that before or after he pins a medal on me?"

"Good point," Maddux said. "Let's go home."

MADDUX CHECKED OVER his report one last time before walking it down the hall and delivering it to Pritchett. Getting captured along with failing to return Dr. Schwarz on the first attempt wasn't exactly a shining moment for Maddux. But he figured the end result would trump any shortcomings on the operation. If he wanted to drill down into the reason why he didn't succeed, he could point to inept technology. However, he would never do that to Rose, especially after what she did for him.

As Maddux strode down the hall, he couldn't help but smile. The operation had ultimately gone as planned—Dr. Schwarz was back at Langley, working with the space program, and Dex and Fulbright were home safely. The lone wrinkle in everything was the blown cover of the two CIA agents who would have to be relocated to a different station in another part of the world.

"You did it, pal," Dex said as Maddux walked by.

He stopped and glanced over his shoulder, catching Dex's eye before seeing Rose.

"No," Maddux said, "actually, *she* did it. You can thank her for pulling this whole thing off."

Maddux breezed up to Pritchett's open door, knocking on the jamb before stepping inside. Pritchett was turned around, pecking away with his good hand on his typewriter. He didn't pause to see who it was but started talking anyway.

"You'd think by now someone would have invented one of these things for people with one hand," Pritchett groused. "I'm hovering all over the board like I'm working a Ouija board."

"If it's any consolation to you, sir, that's how it is for those of us with two hands who have to hunt and peck," Maddux said.

Pritchett spun around in his chair and faced his visitor. "I hope you have that report you promised me."

"It's right here," Maddux said, tossing the document onto the desk.

"I thought I was never going to get to read what actually happened over there. I was sitting here wondering if you were ever going to come back alive."

"Then that would've made two of us. I was just hoping they let me live."

"Well, since Mr. Jim Whittaker was only in the Bonn office files, we've made changes to our protocol when working with civilian assets and their employers. From now on, corporate headquarters will also be adding aliases to their payroll list."

"I'm glad something good came out of that whole debacle."

"In the meantime, you managed to keep your cover," Pritchett said. "According to our sources, the

East Germans just thought it was a coincidence that you were affiliated with the prison break. Apparently, one Phil Billings was a high value prisoner that they see as the cause for all of the dramatic escape."

"So his last name was Billings?"

"Did you find out much about him?"

Maddux shook his head. "No, but I found out he knew a lot about John Hambrick."

Pritchett's eyebrows shot upward. "Oh, did he now? Where did their paths cross?"

"Berlin and they were working together on some kind of engineering project. He never really said what. But he suggested that he knew quite a bit about John Hambrick and what he was doing today."

"And?"

Maddux looked down and sighed. "He was going to tell me later. I guess whatever Phil knew, he took to the grave with him."

Rose rapped on the door and ducked inside. "Have you told Maddux about the commendation you will receive over all this?"

Maddux's jaw fell agape. "You're getting recognized by the agency?"

Pritchett shrugged. "The agency, the President of the United States, I don't know. It all seems the same to me."

"You sly devil," Maddux said. "LBJ is going to pin a medal to your chest for all this?"

"Well, if I'm being honest, the real medal should be pinned on you two."

Maddux shook his head vigorously.

"No, sir. Not me. Rose was the one who risked

everything to help make this happen."

Pritchett chuckled. "Well, maybe I'll give the medal to her then."

"She certainly deserves it," Maddux said.

Rose waved them off dismissively. "Stop it, you two. I'm going to turn red in a moment. I was just doing my job."

Pritchett grunted. "That's not your job, Rose, and you know it. You got lucky this time, and I'm not going to complain about the results. But please don't let that happen again. If you have an idea, bring it to me and let's talk about it. Don't just go skipping off to some country because you think my job needs saving."

She crossed her arms and huffed. "Look at me and tell me that you think you would've survived this post if we hadn't rescued Dr. Schwarz."

"I can't lie. I would've been sacked by Director Raborn at worst, reassigned at best. I would've been that curmudgeon everyone feels sorry for."

"Exactly," Rose said. "We are a family here, and we stick up for each other. And I'm not about to apologize for anything I did or change the way I operate."

Pritchett chuckled, closing his eye and shaking his head as he did. "Okay, point taken. I won't mention it again. You went above and beyond and did a great job. Just let me know what you're doing next time."

"Roger that," she said.

Maddux explained he needed to get back to his duties at Opel. After Maddux had exited the office, Rose chased after him.

"Ed," she began, "where are you going in such a hurry?"

"I have a lot of work to catch up on."

"Okay," she said. "Maybe we could do dinner tonight."

"I'd like that," Maddux said. "Besides, I need to properly thank you for what you did in coming after me like that. I know you said it was for Dr. Schwarz, but I can't help but think you had some other motives for risking everything like you did."

She smiled and turned a shade of red. "I admit, there may have been some other factors involved."

"Well, I look forward to discussing them with you this evening," Maddux said before turning to leave.

On his way out the door, one of the mail clerks flagged Maddux down.

"Sir, a letter came for you today," the clerk said.

"For me?" Maddux asked.

"You're Ed Maddux, aren't you?"

He nodded. "In the flesh."

"Well then, this letter is for you."

Taking the envelope, Maddux shoved it into his pocket. He decided not to open the letter until he was sitting down in his office. The handwriting didn't look familiar, causing Maddux not to take the letter seriously.

When he reached his desk, Maddux settled into his seat. He leaned back in his chair and pulled out the letter opener from his top drawer. After sliding the blade across the top of the envelope, he retrieved the letter.

"What's this?" he said aloud.

The name scrawled in the upper corner was Phil Billings.

Is he alive?

Maddux read the letter intently, learning that Phil

had managed to survive by convincing the East German officers on site that he had been forced to participate in the heist. He offered to investigate the wall later that evening, taking the opportunity to disappear into the wreckage and emerge on the West German side. Phil thanked Maddux for listening to him while they were in prison and also included some other interesting facts about John Hambrick.

"I know why you care so much about any information related to John," Phil wrote. "It didn't take me long to see the resemblance. You're seeking your father, which I think is commendable. But be careful. Your father isn't to be trusted, not because he isn't a good man, but because he is."

What the hell does that mean?

Maddux scratched his head over Phil's cryptic message. Trying to make sense of it all hurt Maddux's brain. But he didn't mind too much. His father was still very much alive—and very much an important person in both the U.S. and Russia.

And Maddux couldn't wait to learn more.

THE END

ACKNOWLEDGMENTS

Starting a new series is always frightening territory for an author. Until readers start tearing into a story, I always wonder if they are going to resonate with my characters and with the storyline. So far, the feedback I've received on the first book in the Ed Maddux series has been encouraging, and I hope that continues as the series progresses.

The bulk of my research for this novel took place at the National Archives, and I'm incredibly grateful to Steven Hamilton for his direction there. Finding these CIA papers from the 1960s wasn't easy, and I doubt I would've ever thought to look for them had it not been for him.

As usual, I appreciate the editing skills of Krystal Wade in making sure this book is fit for publication.

And as always, I must thank my wife for listening to me babble on about espionage while I worked away on crafting this story.

Last but not least, I want to thank you, the reader, for supporting my work. I hope you enjoyed reading this book as much as I enjoyed writing it.

ABOUT THE AUTHOR

R.J. PATTERSON is an award-winning writer living in the Pacific Northwest. He first began his illustrious writing career as a sports journalist, recording his exploits on the soccer fields in England as a young boy. Then when his father told him that people would pay him to watch sports if he would write about what he saw, he went all in. He landed his first writing job at age 15 as a sports writer for a daily newspaper in Orangeburg, S.C. He later attended earned a degree in newspaper journalism from the University of Georgia, where he took a job covering high school sports for the award-winning *Athens Banner-Herald* and *Daily News*.

He later became the sports editor of *The Valdosta Daily Times* before working in the magazine world as an editor and freelance journalist. He has won numerous writing awards, including a national award for his investigative reporting on a sordid tale surrounding an NCAA investigation over the University of Georgia football program.

R.J. enjoys the great outdoors of the Northwest while living there with his wife and four children. He still follows sports closely and enjoys coaching his daughter's soccer team.

He also loves connecting with readers and would love to hear from you. To stay updated about future projects, connect with him over Facebook, on Twitter or Instagram (@MrRJPatterson) or on the interwebs at:

www.RJPbooks.com